Badger's Wood

BADGER'S
WOOD

by ELLESTON TREVOR

Illustrated by LESLIE ATKINSON

CRITERION BOOKS   NEW YORK

MANUFACTURED IN THE UNITED STATES OF AMERICA

TO

MY MOTHER

Contents

Contents

Badger's Wood

The Broken Water-Wheel

Old Stripe, the Badger of Badger's Beech, was just taking his kettle off the hob because he didn't need it there any more, when there came to his ears the sound of knocking upon his front door. So he put his kettle back on the hob. If there was a knocking, then there would assuredly be a visitor; and if there was a visitor, then he'd surely be wanting a nice hot cup-of-something to be going on with; and the only way of making a nice hot cup-of-anything was to work the kettle into the right mood, on top of the little hot hob.

Within a moment of his replacing it there, it began its comfortable, here-we-go-again sort of delightful singing-sound; while Old Stripe called out:

"Come in, do!"

But no folk did, for a while. They were so long about it, indeed, that the Badger crossed his sitting-room and stood at the bottom of the wide staircase leading up to his front door.

"Come down, do!" he invited; after which he stood and listened there for folk to do as they were so kindly invited. But they never did. They knocked again, instead.

I

"Oh bless me whiskers . . ." murmured Stripe, and began slowly to climb his many stairs, just as generations of his Badgery ancestors had done when *they* had gone to answer the door to *their* visitors. When he reached the top stair, he stood for a moment to allow himself to get over all the others, which were rather steep; then he opened his front door.

"Ah," said his visitor.

"Well, well," acknowledged Old Stripe, and blinked slowly at the folk who stood there. "Are you feeling a little deaf, old fellow, or is it perhaps that you maybe can't hear very well, over-much?"

"Why?" asked Potter-the-Otter with a sigh. "Was there anything especially to hear?"

Old Stripe shook his head, holding his front door wide open for such folk as hard-of-hearing Otters to pass inside.

"Not much, especially," he replied. "I've been shouting about the place for a while, that's all. Calling 'Come in, do!' and 'Come down, do!' and that sort of thing. But since you didn't, here I am. How are you?"

"Middling," said Potter, coming inside and looking highly dismal. "Not so very middling as I'd like to be, but you can't have it all ways." He raised his brown furry head a little and, very politely and in a genteel and mannerly way, sniffed. After he had done this, and had come to his conclusions about it all, he added: "Something c-cooking, I'll b-be bound . . ."

His dismal expression was fading; and in its place

2

there was spreading a happier, more excited kind of look. His eyes grew brighter; and his nose wrinkled a little; and his whiskers began to tremble, very slightly, at the tips. The smell of something cooking always took Potter-the-Otter that way. As Old Stripe had once declared, he had a proper old stummick on him, had Potter-folk, no matter what they said contrariwise. Apart from which, Potter-the-Otter always stuttered whenever he had greed coming on.

"D-definitely s-something c-c-cooking," he nodded, much happier.

Old Stripe gave a quiet chuckle and began going down all his stairs.

"Come along, Potter-folk. There *is* something cooking, and you shall be the first to taste it. Just what it's most likely to be I can't think, but I certainly remember putting *something* in the oven, not so very long ago."

When Potter was halfway down the stairs, he said: "It's pancakes." And he stopped to think about them, and how they'd go *flop* on to the platter and sit there, quiet and sizzly and golden-brown.

"You don't cook pancakes in an oven," pointed out his host. "You cook pancakes in a cake-cooking-pan, that's where you have to do *that*."

When Potter had started off again and had arrived at the bottom of the stairs, he stopped, and announced: "Then it's honey-biscuits baking, that's what it is."

Thinking much about these pleasant and tasty things, he heard Old Stripe's tones coming slowly through his tasty thoughts:

3

"I ran out of honey, Tuesday, so it can't be that."

Potter wrinkled his nose again to see if it could tell any better with wrinkles in it, and at last stood in the sitting-room of Badger's Beech, while Old Stripe followed the appetising smell with his own wrinkled nose; and came to it at last.

"Then I don't know *what* it is," said Potter.

"I do," murmured Stripe, lifting his little kettle and observing it slowly. "I've been putting my kettle down on the pantry shelf, that's just about what I've been doing, by mistake or something unbeknown like that; and it's got some treacle on the bottom of it, which must have got itself on to the shelf as well, unmeaning-to. And now the treacle has gone very hot because of the hob. That's what the smell is."

He placed the kettle back on the hob, and for a moment he and his visitor stood sniffing at the smell it made, for it was pleasant.

"Well," sighed Potter at last, his expression becoming dismal again, "perhaps there'll be pancakes the next time I call. Or maybe honey-biscuits baking."

"You never can tell," agreed Old Stripe. "I'm sorry you're disappointed, I'm sure. But you can't very well eat treacle off a kettle-bottom."

"I'm always a one to try anything," said Potter, wondering how much too hot the kettle-bottom would be for his tongue.

"I know you are," grunted the Badger, "and you'll get into trouble *one* day, with that appetite of yours. Have some nice hot dandelion-coffee, with cream in it, instead of some treacly-kettle-bottom."

4

"C-coffee and c-cream," declared Potter-the-Otter, "is just the s-sort of stuff to t-take away a d-disappointment such as I've just received. Thank you, I'm sure, I will."

"Good," nodded Old Stripe; and within a few minutes his morning visitor was sat down with a steaming jug of golden-brown, bubbly, roasty-scented coffee in front of him; and a cup and a saucer to attend to it with.

"Now," said his host, as he poured out, "what did you come a-knocking at my front door so dismal about?"

"Dismal?" enquired Potter, sipping his golden-brown brew.

"Miserable, you looked," nodded Old Stripe.

"Miserable?" murmured his friend, licking his saucer politely where he had spilled some coffee.

"Face like a pancake," nodded Stripe, not wishing to beat about the bush.

Potter-the-Otter thought about all the things he might be dismal and miserable and face-like-a-pancake about; and when he'd remembered, he looked at Old Stripe suddenly over the rim of his cup and said:

"Oh—*that!*"

Old Stripe nodded slowly.

"That," he said simply.

And sure enough, Potter was looking wretched again.

"Something dreadful's occurred," he said. "That's what I came about. Something horrid. So I came

along to ask you to console me, and—and look into
things for me."

"Ah . . ." nodded his host; and for a moment they
sat in silence, drinking their coffee and having some
more and stirring their blobs of cream into it carefully.
Three or four spring sunbeams were slanting into the
ancient room; and between two of the great brown
beams of the ceiling there sat a spider, spinning himself a new morning web. In the big, wheel-back chair,
Potter-the-Otter leaned comfortably, supping his
coffee; while in the other chair, with his feet tucked
snugly on the rung, sat Old Stripe, waiting to hear
what his friend from the Wild River had to say about
his troubles. At last the river-folk said:

"It's my water-wheel, Stripey."

"What is?" asked his black-and-white-browed host.

"It's been broken."

"Broken?" Stripe blinked in bewilderment.

"Bent," added Potter dismally. "In the night."

"In the night?" frowned the Badger. "But this is
most serious!"

"That's why I came along, because only you, of
all the folk in Deep Wood, could realise just how
serious a thing it is for an Otter to have a broken
water-wheel."

"How did it happen?"

"I don't know. I just went diving into the river,
first thing this morning, for my early bath; and I
noticed something very peculiar. My wheel wasn't
turning."

"No?" Old Stripe sipped his coffee with a deep

6

frown, so that his black-and-white brow was deeply furrowed, as well as striped.

"No," Potter shook his head sadly. "And when I swam over to look at it, I saw it was broken. Splintered and bent, all over. I can tell you, Stripe, I felt *miserous*."

"I should think you did!"

"So I came along to tell you how miserous I felt," said Potter, "because you're just the sort of folk to come along to, in times of trouble and—and crisis."

Old Stripe sighed deeply, finished his fourth cup of coffee, and wiped his whiskers politely on the back of his paw. He usually used the tip of his tail for this, when in company; but he was sitting on that, just now.

"We'd better go along," he declared, "and see what's what, and how it got like it."

"I hoped you'd want to do that," said Potter, a little more cheerfully.

"Then here we go," nodded the Badger; and, a moment later, there they went: up the wide staircase, out of the front door and along the sunlit pathway that wound through the heart of the Wood. Past the turning to Deep Wood Store, where Mr. and Mrs. Nibble kept their shop; round by Woo's glade, where Woo Owl lived in Owl's Beech; down through the depths of Thorny Copse went Potter-the-Otter and his best friend, Old Stripe; until they reached the quiet banks of the river, where the sun sent flickers of feathery light from the winking, twinkling ripples.

By the bank was moored the *Bunty*, the small blue boat that had been built, many a year ago, by Otter

7

himself, for plying between Otter's Island and the mainland of the Wood.

While the Badger sat himself down in the stern, his friend the river-dweller drew in the rope and took the oars, dipping them with an expert paw and pulling away, across the rippling mainwater to the Island. This small green mound of land was set in the middle of the river, at a place where the banks widened, and upon the Island stood the little stone-built house, where Potter-the-Otter lived, and kept his potter's wheel to make pots and jugs and platters and mugs, for the use of all his friends.

This morning, the Otter did not moor the boat, nor did he invite his good friend ashore. Instead, he made round the west bank of the Island, and turned the boat into the wide creek, wherein was built the water-wheel. It was this wheel that turned the potter's stone, driving it through a shaft of stout timber that passed through a hole in the wall of the house. It was this wheel, however, that now had stopped its turning; and Old Stripe could see in an instant that what the Otter had told him was true enough.

"You see?" said Potter, letting his boat ride the ripples without moving. Old Stripe saw, indeed he did.

"Bless me whiskers, Potter-folk," he said, astonished, "it looks as though that wheel is never going to turn again!"

For where there had been strong wooden vanes, were now stumps and splinters; and where there had been the long, straight shaft, was now a broken

8

wreckage. Old Stripe, who knew well enough what the water-wheel meant to Potter-the-Otter, gazed full sadly at this unhappy state of affairs; and, when he had got over his amazement, he said slowly:

"Potter-the-Otter . . ."

"Yes?" asked he.

"Potter-the-Otter," repeated Old Stripe slowly and with a tone of high determination, "something will have to be *done* about *that*."

Potter-the-Otter nodded, with much relief.

"I—I was *hoping* you'd say that, Old Stripe," he said.

"Well," replied the Badger, "I have."

They gazed a moment more at the broken water-wheel.

"And the next thing," said Old Stripe gravely, "is to think out *what* must be done."

Without saying more, Potter-folk looked at his splintered water-wheel; then he looked at his furry old friend from Badger's Beech; and he felt very warm, right down inside him, that there was such a folk as Old Stripe in the Wood, who *knew* what it *meant* to a folk who'd had a tragedy come to him like this.

CHAPTER TWO

Conference at Owl's Beech

Benjamin Aloysius Pomeroy Mole stood on the path beside his bean-patch, and looked at his bean-patch slowly.

The morning air was sunny; and flecks of pollen, and tiny seed-cases, and other woodland flotsam floated among the sunbeams on a gentle breeze. The morning air was quiet; though from Dingle Copse there came to the ears of Mole the morning greeting of the Squirrel there, the Resident Squirrel of Dingle Copse, who was hailing a passer-by. The morning air was warm; and from the depths of some dock-leaves came the dry sound of a beetle-folk as he came forth to sunbathe on the moss.

The morning air, indeed, was delightful in many ways, and delicious in many others; but for Benjamin Aloysius Pomeroy Mole it was also bewildering and shocking. For, as he gazed at his bean-patch, he tried to think what could have happened to it in the night.

"Some wandering vagrant, I suppose," sighed Mole.

For there were no beans left in the patch; there were only a few sticks, and some torn roots, and a bit of leaf-mould here and there.

"Some clumsy traveller, I reckon," declared Mole, "been clumping and stomping all over my best beans." He blinked in the warm sunshine, and half a tear glistened in his eye; because he had liked his beans, very well. Then with a small sniff the tear vanished, and Mole turned along the pathway towards Badger's Beech. Someone must know about what had happened in the night; and Old Stripe was the best folk to tell, because he always knew just how to console a folk who was in trouble.

Mole did not have to walk far, for Mole Mound, where he lived, was the house adjoining Badger's Beech. In fact, there was a certain door in the wall of Old Stripe's sitting-room that led you, if you were to open it, into the sitting-room belonging to Mole Mound. So Mole only had to go from his bean-patch, round the bend of the garden-path, and across the lawn to Old Stripe's squash-bed, to arrive at Old Stripe's back door. There he stood a-knocking for quite a time; and when no-folk had answered, he went round to the door at the front of the Beech. But no-folk was bothering to answer front doors, any more than they were answering back ones. It seemed, in fact, that Old Stripe was not in.

"Oh, blow," murmured Mole, and turned away down along the sunny woodland path. "Bean-patches all stomped upon, and Badgers not at home—there's a fine old beginning for a spring morning!"

With his small pink feet treading softly over the bare earth of the path, where it ran between cushions of emerald-bright moss, he made his way towards the river. If Old Stripe was out, then the most likely place to find him was on Otter's Island, because that was where his best friend lived. But as he neared the path which led to Woo Owl's glade, Mole stopped. There were voices, carrying to his ears on the soft warm breeze. Voices, he'd be bound, from Owl's Beech.

Mole wandered off through the avenue of larches and in a moment was in the quiet clearing where stood the ancient beech in which Woo was Resident. Already the voices had become very much clearer; and Mole was able to tell Old Stripe's gruff, mumbly tones, the higher, more excited murmurings of Potter-the-Otter, and the deeper, booming note of Woo Owl's mellow voice; so that Mole felt cheered, hearing so many of his good friends near at hand.

He came to the bottom of the mighty tree-trunk, whose timber ran upwards almost to the clouds before it became a massy canopy of leaves; and he found the bottom of the wooden ladder that was fixed firmly to the tree. There was a notice, reading:

VISITORING LADER,

FOR FOLK UNABEL TO FLIE

Which included, of course, Mole; for he was visitoring, and couldn't fly. His pink toes curled cautiously round each rung as he climbed them one by one. His large pink paws hauled him up, slowly and carefully, while he tried to keep his black velvet middle from rubbing against the rungs (for he was plump, was Mole). His small pink tongue had come out, to help him concentrate the better; and his tail, which was scarcely of a size to be noticed, trembled to itself with the effort of going up the visitoring ladder.

The mossy floor of the glade was left behind him; and he was higher than the tallest grasses. The ladder moved a little, where the wooden pegs had become loosened by so many visitors; and he was higher than the tallest bushes. And by the time he had managed to get past the rung that was always missing, he could look down and see the top of a young silver-birch; though he looked up again very hastily because of getting dizzied. At last he reached the wide bough that formed the porch outside Woo Owl's front door.

In the ordinary way, Mole would have lifted the knocker and knocked with it, being a visiting-folk. But this morning the door was wide open, and it was impossible to lift the knocker without going half-way inside the hall. Since folk should never enter another folk's house without so much as knocking, Mole called:

"Hoi!" and waited. When no one had said "hoi!" back to him, he called out: "It's me!" But nobody said "is it?" or "well I never!" or anything greety like that. In the end he worked his velvet chest up into a very breathy state, and shouted: "Woo Owl, are you in?"

He knew very well that Woo Owl *was*, because he could hear his boomy tones inside; but it seemed the proper kind of question to ask, at a time such as this.

And it seemed he was right, because a moment later he heard:

"Good morning!" That was Woo's voice.

"Good morning!" replied Mole, and stood impatiently on the porch. It was all very difficult. When a door was shut, you could just knock, and whoever-was-at-home would come and answer you; but when the door was open, and you had to shout things, it was all very confusing.

"How are you?" came Woo's voice politely.

"Oh," called Mole, "I'm all right, thank you, I'm sure!"

And he blinked inside the hallway, where his own plump shadow was standing in the sunbeams. He was just thinking of going away and starting all over again (in case he might find the door *shut* when he returned), when he remembered that it would mean having to go all the way down the ladder, and then all the way up again (which was worse). And, at the same moment, he heard a noise from inside the house; and Woo Owl came out of the sitting-room.

"Oh," said Woo largely, "so it's you, Digger Mole!"

"That's right," said Mole.

"Why don't you come right along inside, my dear fellow?" invited Woo, who couldn't see his visitor very well because the sun was in his eyes.

"I haven't been asked," Mole pointed out simply.

"I must apologise," nodded Woo. "The fact is, my dear Digger, that I was having a Conference. Please step inside and join us, do."

Mole sighed with relief. It seemed a very long time

since he had begun climbing the visitors' ladder; but here he was at last, an official Visitor, being asked inside.

"Conference?" he enquired, following Owl into the great round sitting-room.

"Conference," nodded Woo largely, indicating the smallest chair in the room.

"Hello, Digger!" Old Stripe greeted him.

"Hello, Old Stripe," replied Mole, sitting himself down in the smallest chair (and even then it was rather large for him, he being a modest-sized sort of folk).

"Our Conference," began Woo Owl importantly, "is——"

"Hello, Moley!" said Potter-the-Otter, looking up from his pot of honey-brew.

"Our Conference," began Woo again, "concerns——"

"Hello, Potter," responded Digger Mole, nodding politely to Potter.

"Our *Con*ference," boomed Woo Owl, passing Mole a small brown earthenware pot, "is about Potter-the-Otter's water-wheel," he went on, bringing the flagon of honey-brew and pouring a potful into Digger Mole's pot, "which is broken," he continued. "Try some of that," he added, "I made it last summer, and it is just about right by now."

Digger Mole lifted the little brown pot, and sipped at it slowly. The amber liquid ran over his tongue, and went round inside his mouth, mellow and sweet and delightful.

16

"It's the very best honey-brew," he said truthfully, with a golden bead of it winking upon his left lower whisker, "as ever I've tasted in all me days!"

"Good," nodded Woo comfortably. "As I was saying, our friend Potter found his water-wheel broken, first thing this morning. Buckled by some unknown paw. Bent by some rascally rapscallion. Rendered utterly unservice—unserv—that is to say rendered quite wonky, by some mysterious bad-folk!"

Mole blinked, hearing this.

"Upon that deplorable matter," added Woo, "is this Conference met, to see what can be done about things."

There was an impressive silence. Digger Mole, already annoyed and saddened by the mysteries concerning his spoiled bean-patch, was bewildered by this news of broken water-wheels. Trouble there was in the Wood, and no mistake.

"Can I say something?" he asked politely, being the newest Member of Woo Owl's Special Conference.

"Pray proceed, my dear Mole."

Mole proceeded. "I have trouble, too," he said.

Old Stripe glanced at his black-and-velvet neighbour. Potter-the-Otter stopped supping at his honey-brew. Woo Owl raised his feathery eyebrows and said:

"*You* have trouble, *too*, my good Digger?"

"It's my bean-patch, yes. Someone's come along in the night and gone stomping all over it. There are no beans left any more."

"Bless my *whiskers*!" declared Stripe.

"Not a s-single b-bean left?" asked Potter, goggling.

"This is dreadful!" boomed Woo Owl. "First a water-wheel, then a bean-patch! What next, I should beg to enquire?"

"N-nothing," said Mole. "I hope," he added. "I came along to find Old Stripe, to tell him about it."

Woo Owl lifted a large and important wing.

"Gentlemen," he announced, "this must be enquired into, without delay! I suggest we repair immediately to Digger Mole's bean-patch!"

Digger Mole shook his head sadly.

"I'm afraid it's quite beyond repair," he said. "Until I can plant a new lot of beans."

Woo Owl observed him carefully.

"I didn't mean that sort of repair, my dear Mole. I meant we should—er—should *proceed*, or—or——"

"You mean 'go'," suggested Old Stripe mildly.

"Exactly! Go!"

"Then that's what we'll do," nodded the Badger as they all rose from their chairs. "It will be much simpler for us to *go* than to *repair* or—erm—*proceed*. . . . Much, yes. Come along, then!"

Woo Owl went with his three friends, thinking it puzzling that he, a learned bird, could seldom seem to find the right *word*; whereas Old Stripe, who made no claim to learning, always seemed to know it.

Digger Mole walked out on to the sunny porch, and swung his plump velvet figure over the edge, where the notice said:

THIS WEIGH FOUR THE LADER—
MIND WHO YOU GO!

—and found himself safely on the rungs. Down he went, paw below paw, while Potter-the-Otter followed, putting his large webbed feet sometimes on the rungs, occasionally on Digger Mole's head, and now and then on Digger Mole's back, while Old Stripe trod twice upon Potter's ears and once upon his whiskers. Last came Woo Owl, clambering slowly and with careful dignity down the shuddering ladder until he remembered his wings, when he simply spread them and drifted solemnly to the moss, to await his friends.

They reached the ground; Old Stripe with a piece of fur missing from his middle (where it had caught in a crack on a rung), Potter-the-Otter with a bent whisker, and small Digger Mole, with an Otter's footprint on the top of his velvety head.

"Now," said Woo loudly, "let us repair to—I mean let us be going!" And, with a series of heavy hops, accompanied by a series of heavy flaps of his wings, he crossed the glade, followed by Stripe, Digger and Potter, plodding along at their best speed.

Before the sunbeams had moved an inch or two round the woodland trees, the four folk stood in Mole's vegetable garden, and looked down at the place where all his beans had been.

"Disgraceful," muttered Stripe, seeing the state of the ground.

"Most horrid," nodded Potter, who was partial to fresh garden beans.

"Highly dismaying," boomed Woo Owl, "in the extreme!"

Old Stripe spoke again, quietly.

"Someone has been in the Wood," he said, as they listened attentively, "and someone has broken old Potter's wheel, and they have torn up all Digger's best beans—now what are we going to do?"

"Investigate!" declared Owl promptly.

"Agreed!" nodded Stripe.

"Ask questions of every folk in the Wood!" said Potter.

"*That's* what we'll do!" agreed Mole.

Woo Owl turned from the bean-patch, set his course for the pathway to Dingle Copse, and said grandly:

"Gentlemen—follow me!"

He set off, waddling pompously and with much important nodding of his feathery old head; while behind him there went Old Stripe, a deep frown furrowing his black-and-white brows, Potter-the-Otter, with a worried expression on his shiny-brown whiskers, and Digger Benjamin Aloysius Pomeroy Mole.

CHAPTER THREE

The Vanishing of the *Bunty*

None in the Wood could tell Woo Owl anything about the troubles that had come. The Squirrel of Dingle Copse knew nothing; nor did the Raven of Towering Elm. Scruff Fox of Fox End could throw no light upon the matter; nor could the Weasel from Wednesday-hill.

All the day long, Woo and Stripe and Digger and Potter went about the Wood, trying to find someone who could help with the investigation. But no, there was none who could, and none who had seen anything unusual, heard anything mysterious in the night. The mystery remained a mystery; the puzzle grew no clearer.

That night, Old Stripe went home to his bed in Badger's Beech, and dreamed of garden beans, nine in a row. Digger Mole put his small black velvet head upon the pillow in his own Mole Mound, and dreamed of a row of earth, where once had been nine beans. Potter-the-Otter slept to the lullaby of the ripples, and he dreamed of a brand-new water-wheel. Woo Owl pillowed his head on his own soft feathers in Owl's Beech, and dreamed he was leading a Great

Investigation through the Darkest Jungles of North Hickory-land, in search of the missing water-wheels that grew there, nine in a row.

By morning, nothing had been discovered, or solved. The mystery of the bean-patch remained, as did that of Potter's wheel. More than this: there was added a third puzzle, before the sun was higher than the hills.

Last night, Potter-the-Otter had moored the *Bunty* in the small creek of the Island's western shore; this morning, when he had gone to board her and row to the mainland, she was no longer there.

Had Old Stripe taken the boat, after swimming across for it, to go a-rowing down the river? Old Stripe had not, as he told Potter the minute he answered the door. Had Digger Mole gone boating, early on this sunny morning, to work up his appetite for breakfast? Not Mole, said Mole, when Potter called at the Mound to ask him just that question. Woo Owl? "Not I," said he, when Potter knocked upon his lofty door.

They asked everyfolk they knew; but none had borrowed the *Bunty*.

Come lunch-time, Woo Owl took off from his Beech, and flew southwards to where the Wild River passed below the slopes of Heather Hill; after which he swooped low, along the water-course past Marten's Elm, over Otter's Island, round the bend by Stricken Oak, and down to the Silver Falls, where the river forked and plunged to the brink of the rapids. The *Bunty* was never sighted. Woo hovered for a while over the Falls, then folded his wings and dived, down, down, down to where the silver waters tumbled along the bed of the canyon below. But there was no wreckage there. If Potter's boat had drifted from her mooring in the night, to glide over that dizzy brink and crash down to the rocks beneath, there was not a beam or a spar of her left in any crevice that Woo could see from the air.

He made a salad, of the richest things in his pantry, as soon as he returned from his flight; and Potter came to lunch, with Stripe and Digger Mole. Afterwards, they sat upon the lofty balcony near the top of the mighty beech, and Woo Owl gave them tobacco for their small briar pipes, to help them think the better.

Old Stripe sucked quietly at his gnarled old pipe, but nothing came to his mind. Digger Mole sent up a curl of blue and fragrant-scented smoke, but he could think of nothing. Potter-the-Otter just sat and sat, saddened because of his boat; and nothing occurred to him, save that the little blue *Bunty* was lost for ever. At last Woo Owl rose from his chair, and leaned on the rail of the balcony, to gaze down across the Wood to where the Wild River ran between the banks of primroses and purple brook-lime blooms.

"Well, now," he said to his pondering friends, "I'm thinking it must be a boat and a boatman that's been causing all this trouble. That is what I'm thinking." And he puffed again at his corn-cob pipe, to help him puzzle things out.

"A strange sailor-folk?" asked Potter, looking up.

24

Woo nodded slowly.

"I'll tell you why I think it," he said. "In the first place, nobody could have broken your water-wheel except a folk in a boat. Only something as large as that could have done so much damage. If it was a boat, then it wasn't the *Bunty*, or she would have shown the marks on her bows. So it must have been a foreign ship, *I* think."

"A foreign ship . . ." murmured Potter-the-Otter, tilting his head in thought. "A strange sailor, finding his way into the Wild River, you mean?"

"That's just what I mean, old Potter. A sailor who came sailing up the river, and struck your water-wheel in the dark."

Old Stripe watched the blue-drifting smoke from the bowl of his small black pipe.

"*That* seems to be worth thinking on," he declared.

"That is not all," went on Woo Owl. "I think he made a landing, that night, and, being short of stores, went roaming through the wood——"

"——And robbed my bean-patch!" gasped Digger Mole.

"And last night," took up Potter excitedly, "he came up the river again, and stole the *Bunty*!"

There was a breathless pause.

"That's just what I'm thinking," said Owl.

Old Stripe stood up, and leaned with his feathery friend on the rail of the sunlit balcony.

"It all fits in!" he declared. "There must be some sort of sailor——"

"In some sort of foreigner's ship!"

25

"A raider by night!"

"A pirate-folk, maybe!"

Woo Owl went on nodding.

"Then there's only one thing to be done!" said Old Stripe. They looked at him, intently. Though Owl had figured out the cause of these mysteries—if he was right—he had not gone so far as to think of how to stop their happening upon future nights. But Old Stripe, it seemed, had an idea all his own.

"Tell us!" said Mole.

"What should we do?" asked Potter.

"Well, Old Stripe?" said Woo.

"Build another boat," said the Badger from Badger's Beech. For a moment they were silent, thinking about doing this. Then Digger Mole nodded, eagerly.

"A new boat," he said, "to guard our shores!"

"A ship to defend the mainland!" cried Potter.

"In which we can stand-by to repel boarders!" added Old Stripe, who had once heard a Sailor-Rat use those very words at the top of his swashbuckling voice.

"Bless me velvet," cried Mole, "we'll build a fleet!"

Woo Owl regarded them quietly.

"No need for a fleet, my dear Mole," he said. "With one ship we can hunt the raider on his own ground— or on his own water, I should say."

"On *our* own water," suggested Potter warmly; for the Otters had dwelled upon Otter's Island ever since the Wild River first found its winding way among the timbers of the Wood.

"And how long is it going to take us," enquired Old Stripe (for nobody else had thought of it), "to build a new boat?"

Potter-the-Otter put his furry brown head on one side, and said: "We-ell, now—maybe three or four days. We shan't be bothering about any plans or designs, for if I can't raise a good ship from out of me own head, then I'm no river-folk."

"Mr. Nibble will have all the timber we need," nodded Digger Mole. Digger Mole was worrying no longer about his bean-patch. There was a ship to be built; and, though he couldn't confess it to his friends, ship-building was a thing he could grow so excited about that nothing else mattered to him at all.

"Plenty of ash, ay," said Potter, "some good beech, too, Mr. Nibble's got in that timber-yard o' his. Will you all be giving me a paw with the work?"

"*I* shall!" spoke Old Stripe readily.

"M-me, please!" gasped Digger Mole, scarcely knowing how to contain himself. Digger Mole: *Shipbuilder* . . .

"I shall be only too gratified," announced Woo Owl carefully, "to avail myself of the opportunity of offering my assistance in this project."

A small silence fell as they looked at him, frowning.

"Yes," said Potter, "but will you help build our boat?"

"My dear old Otter," said Woo, wondering where he had gone wrong, "that is precisely what I said."

"No," Potter shook his head, "you said nothing about building boats, old Woo; but if you'll help, well,

27

then, we shall get the work done all the quicker."

"We might do it in *three* days," breathed Mole, his small bright eyes shining with shipbuildy thoughts.

"We might," nodded Potter, "for she won't be a big craft, Digger Mole. Seat the four of us, with a light sail and a pair of oars. Simple to build—easy to float—and with a fair turn o' speed about her bows, given a fresh wind . . ."

Mole blinked, and a small tear of utter bliss winked for an instant in his eye.

"All right, then," said Old Stripe, "we'll go along to Deep Wood Store without delay, and if you'll come with me, Potter, you can choose the timber."

"I will," nodded his Ottery friend.

"In the meantime——" began Woo Owl; but Digger Mole, who was dizzy with bliss, piped up:

"Can we build a small *cabin* on the ship?"

"We can," said Potter, "for we'll want some shelter on board if she starts shipping it green."

"And—and a set of lockers?" breathed Mole.

"And a set o' good stout lockers, too," agreed Potter, working it out in his mind.

"In the meantime——" tried Woo again.

"And we'll have a lantern for the front!" cried Mole, interrupting his feathery friend, despite his modest and mannerly ways.

"A lantern for the *bows*, if you *like*," nodded Potter, "for we'll be waiting for the raider-ship by night."

"And we'll have a young fir sapling for the mast!"

"We will," said Potter, as eager as Mole, yet more

thoughtful, for this was a matter close to a river-folk's heart.

"In the meantime——" said Woo patiently.

"And—and a barnacle-lamp," cried Mole, "right at the very top!"

"Or a *binnacle*-lamp," corrected Potter, "if it's on *my* ship . . ."

"In the binnacle-lamp," began Woo loudly and slowly, "I suggest—oh *dear* me, I don't mean in the binnacle-lamp at *all*, I mean in the *meantime* I suggest that I should fly round the Wood——" and he paused a moment, finding that only he was speaking. "Er— I *may* continue?"

"Please do," mumbled Digger Mole humbly, for he could think of no more things that could be built upon their ship.

"Thank you, I'm sure," nodded Woo patiently. "I suggest, then, that while Potter and Stripe are choosing the timber——"

"—And *me*," murmured Mole.

"And *you*," nodded Woo carefully, "while Stripe and Potter and YOU are choosing the timber in Mr. Nibble's yard, I shall fly round the Wood and warn all the folk about what's doing."

"Warn them?" enquired Old Stripe, tapping out his pipe on the balcony-rail and watching the ash floating down to the top of a wild-raspberry bush below.

"Well," said Woo, "I mean that we never know when the raider might strike again—or where."

"You mean," said Potter, "that we should all take

it in turns to mount guard, every night, until we can sail the river in the new boat."

Woo Owl nodded deedily.

"That," he declared, "is my suggestion."

Old Stripe stropped his whiskers with his paw, in a getting-ready kind of manner.

"Then that's what we shall do," he said. "We'll sort out the timber for the boat, and bring it to the Island in Mr. Nibble's barrow; Woo Owl will go round the Wood with his message; and this evening we shall decide who is going to mount guard, and where, and—and that sort of thus."

"Agreed," intoned Woo, and shook out his wings to stretch them, ready for his flight.

"Good!" nodded Potter-the-Otter.

"Then—then c-come along, do!" piped Mole; and he vanished through the door into the beech-tree house, followed by a small velvet draught, and, a moment later, by his three good friends.

The moment for action had come at last, and time was not to be lost.

CHAPTER FOUR

Warning in the Wood

Through the long hours of the afternoon, while the wind came running from the west and the sun shone down upon grass and leaf and moss and winding path, there was much activity in the Wood.

Timber was chosen for the new boat, in the yard behind Deep Wood Store. While Mr. Nibble, the gruff old Rabbit, showed his friends a selection of wood, Potter-the-Otter looked at the lengths of beech and murmured, "ah . . ." and tilted his head at the pile of yew and muttered "umm . . ." and stroked the smooth planks of ash with a knowing paw with a slow and considering "we-ell now . . ." until the time came when the timber was chosen, and piled near the wall of the snug little shop.

"You'll be wanting my barrow," grunted Old Nibble, as he gazed at the rich grain of the wood they were taking. It would make a fine boat, would that timber.

"We'll be wanting that," nodded Old Stripe, "if you can spare it."

"And you'll be needin' some pegs and some nails," he said, half-asleep in the sunshine (for he was very old).

"We'll take some, if we may," said Potter.

"And what about caulking? And pitch? And canvas, and mallets and cleats?" (For he was not altogether asleep, old though he might be; he knew how a ship must be built, did quiet Old Nibble.)

"I've plenty of pitch," said Potter, "but we'll want canvas, ay."

So, when Nibble had woken his other half up, and collected his wits together, he found some canvas and a couple of mallets, and dumped them into his barrow.

"You'd best mind how you go with that," he told them, pointing to the barrow with his old clay pipe. "That wheel, there, that was fashioned before my time, and it gets the tweezles, it does, when you don't watch out. Sticks, it does, and when it sticks the barrow stops sharp and where are ye then?"

"Where am I then?" asked Potter, thinking it might be important to know.

"Why," said Old Mr. Nibble, filling his pipe with clover-leaf and coltsfoot, "you're over the top and down again, with a lump on your head the size of an egg, and maybe a bruise behind. So watch out that wheel don't go an' tweezle on you, when ye don't remember to look."

"I will," said Potter, wondering if it might be better to carry the timber to the river-bank, and leave the barrow here.

"Mind ye do, then, Potter-folk," nodded Nibble, lighting his pipe in the sunshine.

"We'll watch out!" called Mole, as the three of

them pushed off with the barrow, on their first journey to the stream.

Old Nibble waved a paw to them, half-asleep again.

The three shipbuilders pushed the rickety-rockety barrow with its canvas and mallets and beams and planks, all the way through the windy trees until they reached the river bank. Once or twice the wheel had tried to work itself up into a sudden tweezle; but the Woodlanders had remembered the old folk's warning; and Old Stripe still had no lump on his head the size of an egg; while Potter was not the owner of a bruise behind him; nor was Digger Mole in any way bumped or dinged in any part of his velvet. The wheel had grumbled much about this, bumping and squeaking and rumbling and wincing over the earthen path; but of tweezles there were none. Perhaps it had forgotten how.

"Now then," said Stripe, as they halted the barrow at the river's edge.

"Now then what?" asked Mole, pausing to gather up some more Mole-breath from the sunny air, for he was puffed.

"That's what I mean," said Stripe. "Now then, what next?"

"Easy," said Potter. "We'll simply make a rough raft of the planks, and put the mallets and canvas and other small items on top, and float the whole lot across to the Island."

"Ah," said Stripe.

"I don't think we've still got them," said Mole.

34

"Got what?" enquired Potter, laying the planks side by side on the grass.

"The itums," replied Mole, searching for them in the bottom of the barrow. "I think they've all dropped off on the way."

"What have?" asked Stripe, helping Potter with the planks.

"The ITUMS," said Mole crossly. "What do they look like, would you think?"

"I don't know what you mean," said Potter, too busy with making his raft to worry overmuch about what Mole had lost.

"You said," said Mole, "that we could put the canvas and the mallets and the other ITUMS on top of the raft. But I tell you they've dropped off."

He stopped scratching about in the bottom of the barrow (among all the old chips of wood, dobs of glue, bent nails, broken hammer-handles and last autumn's leaves) and turned towards the path into the Wood. "I'll just have to go back and look for them," he stated.

Potter looked up.

"My dear silly old Mole," he said. "When I said 'items' I meant—well, *things*, and—and bits-and-pieces."

Mole stopped, by putting his small pink feet down firmly on the soft green moss. He looked round at Potter.

"You mean to tell me, Potter," he said carefully, "that an itum isn't a thing at all?"

"It *is* a thing," chimed in Old Stripe, carrying on

35

with helping Potter build the raft, "in a way. A hammer is an item; and a mallet is another one; in fact *every*thing is an item, when you come to think of it."

Mole looked at him slowly.

"Everything?" he asked, deeply puzzled.

Old Stripe nodded.

"Everything you can possibly think of," he said.

Mole thought for a moment.

"Even my left ear?" he asked, "or Potter's tail?"

Old Stripe frowned over this question, for he was beginning to forget the sorts of things that were really items, and the sorts of things that were not.

"Of course," he said confidently, certain that Mole didn't know any different in any case.

Digger Mole turned back, and came slowly over to where the other two were throwing together the raft of loose planks.

"Then," he declared, "all I can say is, that an itum must be a very peculiar tackle." And he nodded firmly.

"Pass me that rope, will you, Moley?" asked Potter; and in a moment Digger Mole had forgotten all about mallets and hammers and his left ear and Potter's tail and other very peculiar tackle, and was helping to build the raft.

A dozen planks were roped together, and a dozen more were placed on top; after which all the other items (that is to say bits-and-pieces) were balanced carefully in a heap.

"There you are," said Potter, "now in with it!"

Old Stripe took one end of the raft, and Digger Mole bent his plump-and-velvet knees and grasped the other, while Potter-the-Otter steadied everything as they lifted the raft from the bank.

"Let it down gently," Potter told them.

"Down we go, Moley," said Stripe, staggering a little.

"Over this way," nodded Mole, tottering slightly.

"Not too fast."

"Gently does it."

"Mind how you——"

"Look out, there——"

"Have a care of my *foot*——"

"Steady!" called Potter: and a moment later the raft, Old Stripe and Digger Mole were in the river, bobbing and splashing in a high old state of confusion.

"Hold it there!" cried the Otter, and dived into the ripples, to rise near one end of the raft. "Now then, you two swim across, while I tow the raft behind me!"

Digger and Stripe released their hold of the timber, and struck out across the current, to climb at last to the sandy shore of Otter's Island. Moments later— for Potter could swim more swiftly than they, and his load made little difference—the river-folk beached his raft. Long before tea-time the planks were spread out on the moss to dry, while the mallets and canvas and other things were collected and sorted out, ready for work to begin.

While the three shipbuilders were making ready on

37

the Island, Woo Owl was flying through the Wood, diving to the ground whenever he sighted a dwelling, or rising to some tree-top house where lived a woodland bird.

He called upon the Weasel in Willow Bank, telling him of the raider that had come in the night. He rose to the lofty cottage of the Marten of Marten's Elm, high above the river's southern curve, and warned him of the foreign ship that was suspected of being about. He swooped to the warm green dell where dwelt the Brothers Stoat, and advised them to bolt and bar their doors this very night, in case the raider came.

He visited the Rooks of Lofty Oak, and the Fox of Acorn Copse; he flew to the summit of Cobbler's Hill, and warned the Shoemaker Mole; he called upon every folk in the land, and told his urgent tale.

Evening came.

Upon Otter's Island, Stripe and Mole and Potter and Woo gathered together as the sun went down, and made their plans for the night. Much had already been done towards the safety of the Woodland: a start had been made with the building of the new boat; and Owl had finished his errand among the trees.

If, when night fell, the mysterious raider returned, he would find his stealthy plundering less easy. The Woodland was on the alert.

CHAPTER FIVE

Mole the Miller

No sound was in the Wood, but the wind. No voice was there, not one. Nothing moved, and nothing stirred, for nothing was awake—or so it seemed. The Woodland slumbered, wrapped in a slow mist that was rising from the marshes soft as a blanket of fairy webs, to cover the dells and coppices. Sleep seemed to be everywhere: yet it was not, not quite everywhere.

From high in Towering Elm there watched the Raven's twin and pin-bright eyes. From the depths of Dingle Copse there peered a Squirrel, wide awake. Old Stripe kept his watch at the top of Badger's

Beech. Above Woo's Glade, Owl watched, motionless. On Otter's Island, where the slowly-moving folds of mist crept, white and feather-soft, sat Potter in his boat-shed, with a rug to keep him warm.

No sound came to the Wood. No whisper breathed, no footstep fell; no murmur sounded from the bows of any ship; no flying thing made sighings in the air. The Wood slept, save for these few watchers; but they kept their watch in vain.

Morning came. The first sunbeam slanted from the rim of the eastern hills, and rested golden on the highest elms, the tallest in the Wood.

Old Stripe walked wearily to Otter's Island to report. Digger Mole stretched his plump and velvet limbs, and, with a final peep from the attic window where he had kept good watch, set off towards the Wild River. Woo Owl got up from his wicker-work chair, high on his balcony, and spread his wings.

"Waste o' time, Potter!" he said, landing with a thump of his feet within a yard of his friend's front door.

"Didn't you see anything, Woo Owl?"

"Nothing."

"Nothing at all?"

"Nothing at all whatever!"

"Then come along in for some breakfast," invited the river-dweller, as a shout sounded out from the mainland bank.

"Ahoy the Island! Aho-o-o-y Potter!"

"That's Old Stripe," said Woo; and a moment

40

later there came a splash from the other side, as the Badger of Badger's Beech came to breakfast on the Isle, taking his morning bath on the way across.

"What did you see?" he spluttered, as he came wading up the shore.

"I saw the moon," said Potter.

"I saw the mist," said Woo.

Old Stripe wrung out his tail, and shook the water-beads from his fur.

"I saw no more than you, then," he said.

"Come in for some breakfast," Potter told him, and went inside his house. The kettle was singing and the toast was being made before Digger Mole appeared in the doorway, his velvet winking wet.

"Top o' the morning!" he said busily, wiping a stray water-cress seed from his whiskers. "What news of the night, you folk?"

"Waste o' time," said Woo, and yawned into his wing.

"There's another toasting-fork," Potter pointed, "and there's another loaf of fresh nut-bread. We've wasted our time all the night long, but we're going to make up for it now . . ."

They sat to the long rough-wood table as soon as their breakfast was ready. There were racks of golden-brown toast, and a platter of mushroom-pie; a dish or so of honey-buns and a bowl of cowslip-cream; and to provide an interval (before they began again) they supped a cup of Potter-the-Otter's freshly blended coffee, sweetened with honey and enriched with cream, topped with a curl of steam.

"That," declared Potter, "is better."

"Much better," nodded Old Stripe. "A breakfast, old Potter-folk, such as I've seldom tasted before."

"Then taste it again," said Potter, "there's plenty more."

Digger Mole licked his paw and stroked his chest with it, because of marmalade on the velvet; and when Woo Owl had searched out a missing crumb from the feathers below his beak, he said cheerfully:

"Oh well, he didn't come, whoever-he-was. Never came near us at all."

"Perhaps he won't, again," said Mole.

"Or perhaps he knew we were ready for him," suggested Stripe, looking steadily at the honey-pot. "Er—I wonder if I might just——"

"Do," said Potter, and nudged it towards his friend.

Woo Owl tilted his large feathery head, lifted his large round eyes to the ceiling, and frowned.

"Hark," he said.

They harked, without a sound.

"There it comes again," nodded Owl, and rose from his chair unsteadily.

"There comes what again?" frowned Potter-the-Otter.

"A folk," said Woo, wandering heavily towards the open door. "Calling something."

As Potter and Mole and Stripe followed their sharp-eared neighbour from the house, and stood with him on the moss outside in the light of the rising sun, they heard what he had heard. A faint little voice, calling thinly across the water.

"Hello, Otter's Island! Hello, Potter-the-Otter!"

"Look," said Mole, "it's another one!"

"Another what?" asked Potter, peering.

"Another Me," said Mole, and waved a paw in the air.

The Mole on the mainland bank lifted his own paw, and waggled it urgently.

Woo Owl beat his wings slowly. "I'll fetch him across," he said with a sigh (for he had only just finished his third breakfast). His wings beat faster; and of a sudden he was sailing above the winking ripples of the stream, diving to meet his shadow on the far bank.

"That's Mole-the-Miller," said Digger Mole, "from the windmill on Heather Hill!"

"What can he want?" asked Potter, and went into his house to get some breakfast ready, in case the Miller had not had his yet.

"He seems mightily excited," murmured Old Stripe, as he and Mole watched steadily.

"So would I be," nodded Digger, "if I were to fly across a river on an Owl's back. Most rocky, I should feel."

"What I mean is," persisted Stripe, "that he was highly excited *before* Woo went to fetch him."

"Ah," said Mole, "well, there you are."

Old Stripe observed him carefully, but said no more, until Woo Owl came flying slowly and heavily back from the mainland with his small, black, velvet burden, who was peering from between the wings with a greatly absorbed expression. It was seldom that small Moles flew about the Wood as easily as this; and when they did, they found it a little bit dizzying.

"Steady, Woo!" called Old Stripe, as Owl's large feet were lowered and his wings beat more quickly for the landing.

"Hold hard!" cried Digger; and he and the Badger ran forward, to catch Mole-the-Miller safely, just as he was going to topple from Woo's back and land upside-down on the top of his small milling head.

"Now, then," puffed Woo, regarding his passenger, "what would the trouble be, Mole-the-Miller?"

For a moment the folk from Heather Hill was too busy with excited gulps and unsteady gurgles as he strove to get over his first surprise (which was what he had come about) and then his second surprise (which was flying through the air upon Owl's dipping, diving, swinging, swerving, highly-disturbing feathery back). After a moment he managed; and one pink paw pointed southwards towards the Hill——

"They've gone!" he piped, his paw trembling. "They were there last night and I never gave them another thought until I woke up this morning and had my bath and cooked my breakfast and then went round to the store-room to lift them into the barrow——"

"Oh *please!*" interrupted Old Stripe. "One thing at a time, *please*, and in that order!"

Mole-the-Miller stopped for an instant to gulp.

"Well, they've gone!" he cried. "Four of them—

biggest ones I possessed—held more than any of 'em—
gone! Not a sign to be seen!"

"Bless me front door-knocker," panted Stripe,
"*what* have gone, hey?"

"Have you counted them?" asked Digger.

"If they've gone," pointed out Woo deedily, "he
can't have counted them, can he?"

"Then how do you know there are four?" nodded
Old Stripe.

Mole-the-Miller stared at his audience with wrinkles
in his velvet brow; and when they had finished, he
said:

"Flour sacks."

"Flour sacks?"

"Four flour sacks!" piped the Miller.

"But you don't keep flowers in sacks," muttered
Woo Owl, thinking quietly that too much marmalade
could be a bad thing, on top of too much honey-nut
toast.

But Digger Mole, who, being smallerer, had
enjoyed a more modest breakfast, was clearer in the
head.

"Raise the alarm!" he cried, startling even the
excited Miller.

"Raise the what?" asked Stripe, taken aback.

"Man the pumps!" shrilled Digger Mole, and
pumped the air with his fists.

"*Mole!*" boomed Woo, holding his ears with his
wings, "kindly allow us to enjoy a greater modicum
of silence, if it is at all possible, before we are deafened
by your shrill vociferations!"

"I *beg* pardon?" enquired Digger, stopping his pumping in surprise.

"I invited you," sighed Woo, "to be good enough to——"

"Cease that shocking noise . . ." finished Stripe for him, making it simpler to follow.

"B-But they've been again!" cried Mole. "The Miller has had his sacks of flour stolen in the night! Don't you understand what *that* means?"

"Oh, bless me," muttered Stripe, as he woke up to the point of the matter. "Oh *my* . . ."

Woo Owl uncovered his ears in time to catch Digger's last remark. And he, too, realised, at last, what Mole-the-Miller had come to tell them.

"Oh, *tut!*" he said, his large eyes widening. "Well, *there's* a thing!"

Mole-the-Miller nodded. It seemed that his urgent message was clear at last. But there was more to tell.

"For another thing," he said, brushing some stray flour from his chest and sneezing into the little white cloud, "I know where they've gone, my four flour sacks!"

"You—you do?"

"Where, then?"

"Where have they gone?"

He pointed. "To the river," he said, and nodded.

Old Stripe gazed at the ripples, almost expecting to see four flour sacks a-floating down the stream.

"How d'ye know, Mole-the-Miller?" he asked.

"Simply because," said the milling-folk, "flour is white stuff, flour is, and powdery stuff in addition. It leaves a lot of mess, does flour, wherever you happen to go, if you happen to be carrying some." He banged his middle, which he always used for bumping flour sacks into his barrow after he had lifted them. A cloud arose, and he sneezed into it again, because it was powdery stuff. "You see what I mean?" he said.

"You mean," breathed Digger Mole, "that it leaves a trail!"

"Exactly. A trail. From my mill, right down the path to the bank of the river."

There was a silence, now. The picture was clear, to Woo and Stripe and Digger: the picture of the raider, stealing down Heather Hill in the night, laden with flour sacks, to stow them on his foreign ship, and then to sail away.

"*Potter!*" cried Digger Mole, and within a moment, the river-dweller was out of his doorway.

"There's only one thing to be done!" he said, when he had heard the news.

"Tell us!" piped Digger Mole, dancing a small jig-o'-war on the sunlit moss.

"By tonight," declared Potter, "we must be out along the river, in our new ship! There's only one way to tackle this raider, and that's on the water!"

"Our—n-new ship?" gasped Digger Mole.

"B-but it isn't built, by half!" boomed Woo.

"It will be," said Potter, "if *I* have anything to do with it! We're going to finish that boat by nightfall, if we have to break every hammer and our own backs into the bargain! Who's with me, hey?"

"I am!"

"I'm ready!"

"Show me the way!"

"Hurray for Potter!"

"Down with the pirate!"

"We'll scuttle his ship for him yet!"

And there went Potter, running for the boat-shed, with Woo and Stripe and Digger and Mole-the-Miller hopping and shuffling, skipping and tripping in his wake, to help him build a boat in one short day.

CHAPTER SIX

The Good Ship *Dragonfly*

Potter-the-Otter stood in the doorway of the boat-shed, his paws upon his hips. "What orders, Cap'n Potter?" asked Old Stripe.

"Mole-the-Miller," he told them, "had best go home, for he's got the mill to see to."

"I have," nodded the folk with the flour-white chest, "and, much as I'd like to help with the work down here, it wouldn't be long before you all ran short o' fresh nut bread."

And off he went, upon Woo Owl's feathery back across the river to the mainland shore.

"Old Stripe," said Potter next, "must sleep until noon."

"*Sleep*?" gasped the Badger. "B-but there's a boat to be built!"

"You didn't sleep all night," said Potter firmly, "and if you don't have a doze before this evening you'll either hit your shin with a mallet by mistake because you're too dozy to make out what you're at, or you'll want to go to bed just when we're all ready to launch the boat and sail in search of the foe! Off ye go, now! I'll wake you myself, for lunch!"

Old Stripe turned away, and walked slowly across to the house where Otter lived, bitter disappointment written all over his trousers at the back. It wasn't going to be easy, having to go to sleep when there was a ship being built just outside the window. It wasn't going to be at *all* easy, *that* wasn't going to be.

"Digger," said Potter-the-Otter, "you'll have your sleep between lunch and tea-time, and I'll do the same, while Woo and Stripe can carry on with the work. Then Woo can go to bed from tea until supper, and by that time we shall *all* be feeling fresher for the night."

"All right," said Mole. (By tea-time, he could find some task or other that would keep him out of sight; and then Potter would forget to send him to bed.) "All right," he said. . . .

Potter-the-Otter nodded, as Woo Owl returned from ferrying Mole-the-Miller to the mainland.

"Good. Now then, I'll show you how we go about it!"

For some time, while Digger and Woo listened carefully, Potter-the-Otter talked to them of many different things. There was caulking and pitching, splicing and hitching, bracing and setting the mast; there was grooving and boxing, rigging and chocking, and making the bowsprit fast.

All the time he talked, Potter drew sketches in the sandy shore, with a pointed beam in his paw, while Digger and Woo Owl nodded and tilted their heads and said "yes" and "no" and "what's that bit?" and "*that* looks very difficult" and "oh well, if we get into trouble there's always you . . ."

51

The work began.

An ash-beam was taken, bent and beaten, until it was curved round to join two more. Planks were hammered, snug within grooves, and bent and fixed with pegs, clouted and cut into equal lengths. Joists were struck, and the three mallets beat, beat, beat, clattered and battered, butting the joists to the beam, until it was rigid, strong as the brace of a bridge.

More timber was fetched from Deep Wood Store; more ash, more beech, more yew; more pegs and a new drill; three more mallets, in case these should lose their heads with all the banging and clouting and beating.

The planks and beams and joists were pegged and curved, battened and bowed, fixed and fastened well. They had become a skeleton ship, a frail timbered shell.

Later, when Old Stripe came from the house, rubbing the sleep from his eyes, the timbered shell grew fat, and deep, and wide; and there were bows, and a stern, and port- and starboard-beams. Then they caulked the seams.

Potter and Mole stopped work, in the warmth of the afternoon, while the other two carried on. There were blisters on Digger's large pink paws, and sawdust in his fur; his plump little arms ached till they were hot with ache, and ached till they wouldn't stop. So he was glad enough, was small weary Mole, to go to his bed until tea-time came to fetch him back to work.

The shell that had become greater, had now become a ship. She stood, this ship, just as twilight came falling through the quiet leaves, stood with her bows lifted and her stern full-square on the shore. Her beams were propped with posts until she could be launched. Her mast went up like a tall tree against the pale sky, and from the mast to the prow and the mast to the stern ran rigging, taut as a willow within a wind.

The work was done, by twilight; the ship stood there, in a place on the shore where never before a ship had been seen to stand. A new ship, born with mallets and muscles from the small blue ghost of the *Bunty*. A ship against the raider, ready for the foe.

Old Stripe dropped his tools and sat down on the

moss. Digger Mole put down his ropes, and lay flat on his plump velvet back, so that his face was turned to the cool arch of the sky where now stars winked, staring down as he stared back, weary and flat on his back. Woo Owl leaned, a limp figure of feathers, against the wall of the boat-shed, and mopped his brow with his wing.

Potter said nothing, as he stood quietly a little way up the shore, looking across at the ship. To his friends, good folk of the timber-land, the ship was something that had been made from wood and rope, pitch and beam. But to Potter-the-Otter, in whose warm old heart there was every ripple and every reach of this, his own Wild River, the ship meant more. Since this morning, something had come alive, and stood waiting, eager for the slap of the waves below her bows, ready to strain against the swirl of the current past her keel, longing most of all for the great thrusting of the wind within her canvas, decked to greet it.

Woo Owl gave a sigh, half weariness, half pleasure, and came waddling down the sandy shore.

"Built in one day," he said, shaking his head as though he couldn't believe himself. "Built between dawn and sundown, bless me feathers! And what shall be her name?"

Potter-the-Otter turned at this, and went into his house. When he came out, and joined his friends on the sand, they saw he had a flagon in his paw.

"Blackberry-wine," he said, and slapped the flagon. "We'll launch her with blackberry-wine!" Saying which, he drew the ancient cork, and passed the flagon to Stripe beside him. "You first, Old Stripe!"

The Badger took the flagon, wondering what to do with it. He had a notion that you had to throw the bottle at the bows when you named a fine new ship; but then he wasn't sure.

"Drink up!" said Potter.

So Stripe drank up, for Potter must know the proper way to launch a boat, if anyone did. After him, Digger Mole took a draught of the blackberry-wine, and liked the taste of it well, and enjoyed the way it ran round and round his tongue and down into his middle where it went round—and round—again—with such a warm and pleasury sensation. And when Woo had drunk from the flagon, and Potter had drained it dry, they stood and gazed at their fine new ship. Starlight was on her rigging, and the moon sent a gleam for her mast.

"Well," said Potter, trying to think.

"I can't think of a name," frowned Stripe, "for the life of me I can't."

"Nor me," said Mole.

"The question is difficult," murmured Owl gently, and licked the outside of his beak with his tongue. "Difficult in the extreme."

"She'll have to have a name before tonight," said Potter. "She can't sail against the enemy without a name."

He was just thinking of all the names of ships he had ever heard of, and deciding that none of them would do, when a low murmur of wings

55

sounded softly from the river, and he turned his head.

Slowly, and with delicate movement, the winking blue insect drifted from the reeds, and murmured with its four mazy wings across the sand. The pale moonlight flashed once, and once again upon the blue and gauzy creature, so that its murmuring wings seemed a mist of azure, a haze of blue. Then the sound of it stopped; and stillness came. It vanished across the quiet waterway.

Potter-the-Otter listened, but heard the wings no more. He gazed, holding his breath: but the delicate blue had gone.

"Props away!" he said; and Stripe took a mallet.

"Down she goes, then!" And Woo Owl gave a heave.

"Free!" called Potter, "she runs free!"

And free she ran. Down the slope of the sands, clean into the ripples with a slap of her stern and a shudder in every beam.

"You good ship!" cried Potter, waving the empty flagon high in his paw, "you good ship *Dragonfly*!"

The flagon whirled, and struck the prow, shattering to the shallows; and with a leap, Potter-the-Otter made aboard, running to spread the sail.

"The *Dragonfly*!" called Stripe, waving a boisterous paw.

"The *Dragonfly*!" cried Digger Mole, and made such a merry jig on the shore that his feet were lost in the sand.

"The *Dragonfly*!" rose the booming echo from Woo Owl, as he rose with a beat of his wings.

The Woodland had a ship again. Her beams were true; her mast was tall and slender; her sail was spread to cup the friendly wind; her name was the *Dragonfly*.

CHAPTER SEVEN

The Galleon in the Mist

Three-quarters of the moon was lit; but its light was thin, this night. The mist, that had gathered above the soggy wastes of Winter Marsh at sundown, was now rolling, creeping, moving as a great grey web across the Wild River.

It hid the moon's light, save for a pale glow. It drew its damp and clinging folds across the meadow-land, among the trees, blanketing the water and the land alike, so that a folk who walked abroad in the Wood must surely take care, or find his feet in the river without a second's warning.

Somewhere within the pale grey wastes of the stealing, moving mist, there went a shape. In the great silence, there sounded sometimes the soft lapping of the ripples upon timbered beams, or the faint slapping of canvas as the sail strove to catch the wind— the wind that was not there.

Quiet in the gloom, the ship moved, a shadow within the mist, a wraith along the waterway. There were three on board.

Potter-the-Otter, Cap'n of the *Dragonfly*, sat to the helm, searching the surface of the river with eyes that,

58

keen as they were and well familiar with the scene,
saw nothing but the mist, and the glint of the moon
now and then.

"How far shall we go?" murmured Digger Mole,
perched upon a small rope cradle, halfway up the
mast.

"Past Stricken Oak," said Potter, "and onwards
until we feel the tugging of the current by Silver Falls.
Then we'll come back, as far as Heather Hill."

"Then we'll have to use the oars," muttered Old
Stripe, sitting watchful in the bows. "There's no wind
for the sail, not a breath."

"We'll use the oars," nodded Potter, "as soon as we
turn against the current."

They said no more for a while. Sitting in his rope

cradle that was slung about the mast to make a look-out, Digger Mole kept watch, his short plump arms hooked through the ropes in case he tumbled the ten feet down to the deck, his short plump legs hanging down and swinging to the lazy movement of the ship. Upon his velvet was a sheen of dew, where the myriad tiny beads of the mist were clinging to him. His small bright eyes stared, hardly ever winking, down across the bows to scan the way ahead.

Old Stripe sat on the forward locker, couched on a coil of rope. His little black briar smoking-pipe was in his teeth, but empty of tobacco. The glow of the tinder might be seen if he were to fill and light it; even the faint aroma of the smoke—the warm scent of burning clover-leaf and honeysuckle—might drift above the water and reach the sensitive nose of the enemy, if he were abroad in the mist. So Old Stripe sucked at his pipe, and gazed with an unwinking steadiness that wearied his eyes.

Potter-the-Otter, Captain of the *Dragonfly*, held the helm firm in his paw. He could scarcely see through the rolling mist; and more often than not the banks were hid from his view. Now and then it was necessary for Old Stripe, up in the bows, to guide his captain—

"Starboard a bit, Potter-folk—starboard a point."

The helm swung; the rudder turned; the current tugged and the ripples ran, gurgling and swirling in surprise. The prow came round a bit, round a point to starboard.

Above the course of the winding water there moved another form, silent and soft, yet faster than the drifting *Dragonfly*. Woo Owl was abroad on his downy wings, keeping his watch from the air. At the first glimpse of any foreign ship along the Wild River he would race to the *Dragonfly* with the news; but there was no glimpse, no sight or sound or hint of any foe.

By Winter Marsh his wings took him, silent through the rolling veils of mist; then, as he sighted the shadow on the curve of the river, he swooped, calling softly before he came down on the drifting *Dragonfly*.

"Well, Woo Owl?" asked Potter, gripping the helm in sudden excitement.

"Nothing seen, Cap'n Potter!" said the flying lookout, furling his wings.

"Nothing?" asked Digger Mole, from his perch halfway up the mast.

"From Heather Hill to Silver Falls, not a sign of another ship."

"Then he can't be about tonight," grunted Old Stripe, shifting his position stiffly in the bows.

Potter gave a shrug as Woo Owl sat for a moment to rest his wings.

"Maybe not, Old Stripe," he said quietly, "but we must keep on patrol. He came three nights ago, and struck my water-wheel and raided Digger Mole's bean-patch . . ."

Old Stripe nodded slowly.

"That's true enough," he said. "And two nights ago he made off with the *Bunty*, and last night stole flour from the mill on Heather Hill."

"Three nights running," said Woo, "so why shouldn't the scoundrel come again?"

61

"He might have seen us building the new ship, from the distance," suggested Mole, and added: "if my legs get any colder I shan't be able to feel them, and then I'll trip over them when I walk. . . ."

"I doubt if the building of one ship would keep him away," replied Stripe, getting up from his locker. "Come you down from there, Digger Mole, and let me have a spell."

"Oh, I'm all right," said he, swinging his legs to warm them. "I'm only complaining, to pass the time."

Old Stripe stood below the mast, looking up at the pair of short black velvet legs that dangled there.

"The time will pass," he said, "without your mumbling and grumbling up there like an old velvet-coated scarecrow."

"Fine thing," said Mole. "Fine thing, when a folk volunteers to be look-out, and then gets hisself friz with cold, and then gets told he's a scarecrow. Fine old thing, *that* is."

"Come along down," chuckled Stripe, and stood ready to catch his small friend if he chanced to come down with a bump and by mistake.

"Can't," said Mole. "I'm stuck."

"Then you'll just have to unstick, that's all."

"'Tisn't so easy," retorted the look-out, wriggling free of his rope cradle.

"Too fat," murmured Stripe. "Too much plum-pitty, that's your trouble."

"If you'll stop passing personal remarkings," suggested Digger, freeing one leg from the ropes, "and try to be more helpful and sympathisy," he added, freeing the other leg with a jerk that rocked the rope cradle dangerously, "it would be a much better thing, and besides, I—*hooops!*"

Old Stripe went down with a thump as plump little Mole slipped, grabbed at the rope-ladder, missed it, and fell.

"I'm sorry, I'm sure," he said, getting up from the Badger's head. "I didn't exactly mean to do *that.*"

"If I thought you did," mumbled Old Stripe, rubbing his left ear tenderly, "I wouldn't have forgiven you."

"You're nice and soft, Stripey," declared Mole, going unsteadily into the bows with his legs tottering stiffly. "Much softer than the deck, I'll admit that."

Woo Owl stretched his wings.

"I'll be on my way again," he said, "and I'll pass overhead on my way up-water from the Falls."

"Good luck!" said Potter, as Woo beat his wings. In another moment he was gone, rising into the curtain of mist. The ship drifted on, downwater between the silent, unseen banks. Potter was weary at the helm, and thought much about the cheerful fire he could light in the stone-built house on the Island, and of the steaming honey-brew he could make for himself and his friends. They'd sit and they'd talk, watching the moving flames and supping at their pots, while in the room there'd be the sweet scent of the apple-logs, and the lulling, wreathing smoke from their pipes; and behind them their shadows would sit at their ease upon the wall, supping and smoking too. . . .

"What's that?" piped Mole from the bows—and Potter brought his thoughts back to the present with a flash, while Stripe called out——

"What's what?"

Digger stood upright, peering ahead into the grey gloom of the waterway, and as Potter leapt to his feet, ready to swing the helm over if Digger told him to, Old Stripe stared with widening eyes at the stretch of river ahead——

"B-but *look!*" he said.

The voice of Mole piped up:

"The—the trees are moving, down by Winter Marsh!"

"The t-trees are *what?*" shivered Potter, trying to see a sign of what his friends had glimpsed.

"Two saplings," called Stripe, as he boggled into the mist, "are—are gliding along the bank, and——"

"Cap'n Potter!" sang out Mole, "they're not trees—they're masts! *Masts sighted!*"

Old Stripe stood upright in his rope cradle, clinging to the rungs—"Ship ahead!" he shouted, "ship right in our course!"

"Swing your helm!" cried Digger shrilly, "pull over, pull about, Cap'n!"

And, as Potter kicked the helm with all his strength, hard over to starboard, he saw—and shuddered to see—the shape that was looming from the clouds of mist. A great shape, rising from the water, the shape of a ship, a great ship, twin-masted and fully-rigged and twenty feet high in her bows. . . .

"Hard over!" shrilled Mole, hopping about in the prow.

"She'll run us down!" cried Stripe—"*stand-by for collision!*"

But, as the *Dragonfly* came round, her captain knew that he was too late. The other ship came on, a galleon five times the size of the little *Dragonfly*, dead in the course of the Woodlanders' boat, a mighty, magnificent, terrible sight.

"Jump!" cried Stripe, "*jump for your lives!*"

The ships met, the galleon and the sailing-boat, with a swirl of angry-lashing water and a crash of beam and timber that echoed and roared from bank to bank, from creek to creek, from tree to tree in the shattered silence of the night. . . .

CHAPTER EIGHT

Captive Island

Cap'n Potter hit the water with his paws together and his tail out straight, and struck out strongly. Old Stripe, with his feet caught in the entangling ropes of the look-out cradle, would have fetched himself a dismal bump had not the *Dragonfly* heeled over like a leaf in the wind, slinging him clear. Digger Mole was thrown from the bows, and before he knew where he was, he was there—plunging into the water below.

The sailing-craft shuddered to the mighty impact of the driving galleon's bows, shuddered and then was almost lifted, as her starboard beam shattered and her timbers split, flying into the air and splashing down while the waters roared into her gaping breach. The galleon seemed to shake itself, but her speed scarcely slackened as she drove on, cleaving the water, with her canvas spread above her as a great black cloud.

The *Dragonfly*, built in a day, sailed for barely half a night, was foundering, her timber wrecked, her mast shattered, her sail rent to a rag. Before her captain and his crew had swum to the bank of the river, she was gone, sliding to the bottom without another sound.

With her going, there came a shout, lifting from the decks of the murderous galleon as she drove her way onwards, upstream——

"See them swim, now—see them landlubbers swim for their lives, me lads!"

The shout rang, boisterous and echoing between the river banks, while a gust of laughter rose from the throats of the crew; and the galleon was gone, driving upstream for the Island.

Potter-the-Otter stood on the bank, shaking the water from his fur.

"I'll sink that fine ship o' yours!" he called across the water. "I'll make you swallow more of the river than you've ever sailed on, you brass-voiced rascal!"

But there was no answer. The mist shrouded all sight, all sound. The pirate had gone, with his great two-masted ship.

"Potter, give me a paw!" came a small voice; and Digger Mole blinked up from a ring of ripples, blowing out a fine old spray of river-water.

"Up ye come, Moley!" said Potter, and lent him a strong furry paw. "Where's Old Stripe?"

"Sinking!" came a splutter from nearby, "I think!"

With Digger Mole spread out to dry on the mossy bank, Potter-the-Otter waded down the alder-holts and hauled out his friend from Badger's Beech.

"Th-thank you, I'm sure," gurgled Stripe, and dumped himself on the moss.

"Are you folk all right?" asked Potter anxiously.

"No," complained Mole, "I'm all wet. All wet,

68

all over." And he sat there stroking the water off his gleaming black velvety chest.

"I've got a lot of river," puffed Old Stripe sadly, "a lot too much river, inside." He wrung out his tail, and sat down in the puddle it made, in error. "I wasn't even thirsty, either," he grunted indignantly.

"How are you, Potter?" asked Mole. "Any bones broken?"

"None of mine," replied he, gazing upstream into the mist. "And none o' theirs, either, which is worse!"

"Did you see them?" asked Digger, rolling on his chest to wring the velvet out.

"Ay, three of them!" snorted Old Stripe, "and probably many more below her decks! You saw who their skipper was, Potter-folk?"

Potter nodded slowly, and his voice was quiet.

"I saw," he said, "and I'm ashamed to say it—but he was an Otter—a black Otter." Then his tone grew angry again. "One o' my own kind, running me down on my own mainwater! I'll put paid to that pesky scoundrel if it takes me all my days!"

"We'll help!" cried Digger, as he stropped his whiskers dry.

"So we will!" snorted Stripe. "He had a crew of Rats, did you see them?"

Potter-the-Otter nodded grimly.

"Ay, Old Stripe. Most likely they're from the canals—Water-Rats, they'd be, tired of barge-life. Looking for a bit of excitement, maybe, they've shipped out with that leather-lunged lubber on board his foreign galleon!"

"Well," sighed Digger Mole, happier now that he was covered in dry velvet instead of wet, "it's time we built us another boat. . . ."

Potter shook his head, and a lump came to his throat; but he swallowed it and put it in its place.

"I'm building no more ships for that scoundrel to run down, Digger Mole. The *Dragonfly* was a good craft, and she did her best; but she was caught unawares, that's all."

"Maybe," suggested Stripe quietly, "maybe we'll raise her, tomorrow—or somewhen, and mend the hole in her planks."

"Maybe we'll do that," said Potter.

Before they could say more, there came a rush of wings from the mist; and a shape loomed, diving to the bank.

"Are you folk all right?" panted Woo Owl, landing near them with a sudden thump of his feet.

"Right as a rainbow," said Stripe, wishing they were.

"Been for a swim," said Mole, wishing they hadn't.

"I heard timber smashing," puffed Woo, "and got here as fast as I could—I was up near the old bridge—what happened?"

Potter-the-Otter told him. Woo Owl listened, his eyes wide and cross as he heard of the foreign pirate and his wrecking of the *Dragonfly*.

"They came through the mist," said Potter, "a fine galleon, straight and rigged like a crack man-o'-war, and flying the Jolly Roger! A crew of Water-Rats and a great black Otter as their cap'n, I'm ashamed to say!"

Woo Owl flapped his wings in crossity, stamping his large feet up and down on the moss, and then down and up as he grew crosser still.

"Well, I saw nothing of them," he said, when Potter's tale was told. "There wasn't a glimpse of any ship but yours, anywhere on the mainwater."

"Then they must have moored-up in some creek," said Potter, "and then swung out at us in the mist."

"Which way did they make?" asked Woo.

"Up-river, they went."

"What? Towards your Island, Potter?"

Potter blinked. *That* was something he hadn't thought about.

"Ay, towards the Island," he murmured, "but you don't think they——"

"Come on!" boomed Woo, lifting himself clear of the ground with an urgent flap of his wings. "The Island's unprotected—what if they make a raid!"

Within an instant he was hopping away with his wings beating just enough to carry him along the river bank, and behind him came Old Stripe, struggling along in the draught, and Potter-the-Otter, running as hard as he might. Last came Mole, for Mole had very short plumpitty legs and that made it bad for running, because of their lackage of length. But, by the time his three friends were opposite the Island, Mole was puffing round the last bend in the river bank pathway, and in a few moments had joined them there.

Potter was pointing with his outstretched paw.

"Look *there* . . ." he said, hardly believing his eyes. They looked there, and scarcely believed their own. Against the dark shadow of Otter's Island there stood another: a deeper shadow, with twin masts lifting to the hazy moon. The pirate's galleon rode there, moored to the Island shore.

"Well bless my old back door knocker . . ." breathed Stripe, "if *that* isn't the boldest thing I've seen in all me days . . ."

"A—a foreign ship," whispered Mole, "moored to our own Otter's Island as if she belonged there!"

"The—the——" hooted Woo Owl, trying to find the word; and when he found it, he said it—"the *nerve!*"

Potter-the-Otter gazed at the dark outline of the ship, upon whose rigging the pale moonlight was beginning to gleam, as the mist began lifting from the waterside.

Old Stripe's voice came quietly.

"Are ye going to swim across, old Potter? Because if you are, I'll go with you."

"And I!" cried Mole stoutly.

"I also!" boomed Woo, "or rather I'll fly, because it's quicker, and—and less wetting!"

Potter put his paws upon his hips.

"*Swim?*" he said, "swim to my own Island? I'll see them to the bottom first! They'll send me a boat across, or I'll want to know why not!"

"I'm afraid they'd tell you," murmured Old Stripe; but Potter was raising his voice to a shout across the water——

72

"Ahoy, Pirate! A-hoy the Island!"

His shout echoed from the great beam of the galleon. No answer came back.

"Ahoy, there!" came Potter's call, "come out, you pack o' skinny-fisted cut-throat land-lubbering dogs o' thunder! A-hoy the Island!"

This time there came reply; but no voice sounded across the water...Instead, a small rock came sailing through the clearing folds of mist, and struck the ripples not far from the river's bank, sending up a sudden water-plume.

"They're throwing something!" piped up Digger Mole.

"They're using slings!" cried Old Stripe.

Potter raised his paws in fury.

"I'll give them fire on me from me own Island!" His voice carried with a roar across the water: "Cease your fire, you mean-livered, jelly-legged skulduggering crew o' scoundrels, or I'll sink the lot of you, take my word!"

"Hear hear!" squeaked Mole, wishing he had such a command of language as his nautical friend.

But another rock, a larger one, came hurtling from the Island, to crash against the trunk of a nearby willow.

"Take cover!" boomed Woo, and hopped nimbly back from the bank.

"Under the trees!" shouted Stripe, as a third boulder came singing over the stream, to thud among the reeds.

73

Potter stood his ground, almost speechless with fury. Almost—but not quite:

"Cast off that leaking tub o' yours!" he bellowed with cupped paws, "or I'll come and cut the ropes myself!"

A chorus of boisterous laughter was the answer from the Isle. "Come across, then!" he heard the challenge, "and we'll lend ye a knife for the task!"

"Scupper me," cried Potter, "if I don't do it!"

"Potter!" called Stripe from the shelter of the trees as another rock came slinging across and hit the bank with an ominous thud. "Come back, you ridicklemous folk!"

"Belay me if I don't swim over and——" began the furious river-dweller, but he was cut short as Old Stripe, Woo Owl and Digger Mole rushed at him and hauled him back into the trees by his belt, his arms, and his furry old furious ears.

"You'll have *such* trouble!" Stripe warned him when he was safely out of range of those hurtling rocks.

"If you swim across, you absurd folk," nodded Mole, "you'll only have a rock on top of your foolish head in mid-stream—that's just what they're waiting for!"

"We must treat this—this matter *calmly*," boomed Woo Owl, who was as angry as Potter but just a little wiser in the head. "We must—er—we must apply our reason and our wits to this—this imponderable quandary!"

"I—I beg pardon?" enquired Mole mildly.

"I said," declared Woo, trying to remember all the
words again——

"Yes," broke in Potter impatiently, "but while we
stand here talking, what are those rascals doing?
Rifling my pantry! P-pilfering my p-pies! F-feasting
on my f-fruit and cream!"

"Don't torture yourself, you greedy folk!" said Old
Stripe, laying a paw on his arm.

"We'll get your Island back," said Mole, "*somehow*."

"And we'll do it by making our plans first," nodded
Woo, glad to observe that Potter was calming down
a little. "I think we should all adjourn to my Beech,
and have a council of war there."

"Hear hear!" said Mole.

"I agree!" added Stripe.

"Then we shall retire," said Woo, "to Owl's Beech, and there ponder our peculiar predicament. Come! Let us waste not one moment!"

"What's a predicklement?" murmured Mole, as they turned towards the path.

"A predicament," intoned Woo knowledgeably, "a predicament is a manner of saying—well, it's a sort of—er—*thing*, that one finds——"

"Or loses——" put in Old Stripe.

"Or loses, exactly," agreed Woo.

"Or gets into, unbeknown," suggested Stripe.

"And usually upside-down," Woo nodded.

Digger Mole looked up at the Badger on his left, and then he looked up at the Owl on his right, and after he had thought the matter out very cautiously for a moment, he said:

"So *that's* a predicklement."

"That," Woo told him solemnly, "is a predicament."

"Then," announced small Mole, "I prefer pome-granates, *any* day. Because *they* are *simpler*."

"Here we are," interrupted Stripe, "here's Owl's Beech!"

And, one after another (except for Woo, who flew), they climbed the long visiting ladder, that was there for that very purpose; and long before it had stopped shaking they were in the great round sitting-room, and Woo was putting the kettle on and Stripe was filling his pipe and Potter was going "*humph!*" to himself about pirates being all over his Island, and,

76

in a corner that was just his own size, small black Mole was nodding quietly and saying to himself: "That's what *I* prefer, *any* day." Meaning pomegranates.

CHAPTER NINE

Meeting of the Grand Council

"Who speaks first?" demanded Woo Owl. Round the council-table, Old Stripe sucked at his black briar pipe, and looked at him. Digger Mole sat with his short plump arms folded in front of him, and a most serious expression on his whiskers. Potter-the-Otter looked most serious of all.

Never before had a stranger entered Deep Wood without receiving a welcome. Travellers had come, weary from their journeying, and had found the secluded sanctuary of the trees; and they had not gone their way without a warm bed for the night, and a rich breakfast in Badger's Beech or Mole Mound. Few folk had ever crossed the borders of this secret land, and found their way to its heart; but those who did, returned to their own country with happy thoughts of their friends in the Wood.

But now the raider was here. Wrecking the wheel, plundering the bean-patch, making away with the flour that Mole-the-Miller had ground, stealing the *Bunty*, and, an hour ago on the river, running down another ship—the *Dragonfly*—and sending her crew to the waves. The raider was here, of that there was no doubt.

And the raider must go, as surely as he had come.

"Well," said Woo again, "who speaks first, at this grand council of war?"

"Potter should speak first," replied Old Stripe, "for it's his Island that's in trouble."

Woo and Mole and Stripe turned their heads, and looked at the *Dragonfly*'s captain.

"I don't know," shrugged Potter-the-Otter, "that I've much to say, except that I'm for crossing the water, to tackle them where they stand."

"Too dangerous, Potter," the Badger shook his head.

"I'm not asking any-folk to go with me," put in the river-dweller quickly, "though I know you would, if I did. But as Old Stripe says, it's my Island that's in trouble, and it isn't right that anyone else should have to risk a deal of hurt in the saving of it."

"Twaddle," said Mole rudely.

"Fudge and fiddle," nodded Stripe.

"Pish and—and tosh," agreed Woo Owl. "The Island is your home, Potter-folk, but its soil is ours; it belongs to every one of us, for it's part of our Deep Wood. Am I right?"

"Right!" cried Digger Mole.

"Right you are!" affirmed Old Stripe.

"We relieve the Island together," boomed Woo resolutely, "or we leave it to the foe!"

Potter-the-Otter said nothing. It warmed him to know that his good friends were all about him. A folk, he judged, was never in much trouble, so long as there were friends nearby.

"Now we'll look at Potter's plan," said Woo, "though I must say it doesn't bear inspection. . . ."

"Agreed," nodded Stripe. "They'll be on the watch for us, and as soon as we get halfway across the water, they'll use their slings. Potter might be able to dive and escape the rocks, but we don't swim so well."

"Then," said Potter, "we'll make slings of our own! We'll bend two saplings back and fit a rope between, and send a bombardment of boulders across that'll have them shouting for mercy before we're done with 'em!" He pushed his chair back with a clatter and looked at them in high excitement.

"Sit *down*!" boomed Woo, banging his ale-pot on the table. "This is a council, not—not musical-chairs."

"You're too *rash*, Potter!" nodded Stripe vigorously, as the bold captain sat down slowly. "We can build a great big catapult, yes—but d'ye want to break your windows in and smash your roof and knock all the chimneys down?"

"Then bombard their ship!" spoke up Mole.

"Aye!" responded Potter, "sink their galleon, and leave the rascals wading in the river!"

"I do not agree!" boomed Woo, frowning all over his feathers.

"Nor do I!" said Old Stripe, and added: "Er— why?"

"Because," explained Woo, "if their ship is sunk they will find no option but to remain upon the Island. We shall be no nearer evicting them!"

"I beg pardon?" suggested Mole.

"We shall be no nearer," repeated Woo carefully, "evicting them."

"Ah," said Mole. "Then how *can* we predict them? With a good strong predicklement?"

Woo Owl observed small Mole very slowly indeed; and, after he had committed a large and careful blink, he gave a slight cough, and said:

"Yes. Well, as I was saying, we must think of a better plan." And he paused, listening to hear if Mole was going to trump up any more ridiculous interruptions. But no. Mole was quietly busy, trying to work out how to predict a pirate-folk with a good strong predicklement.

"The only way I can see," suggested Old Stripe, "is by taking their ship away from them, somehow, and making them—making them sort of—of run *after* it."

There fell a short silence. For the first time, it seemed, someone had said something sensible. . . .

"*That* would be all right," mused Potter.

"That would get the ship clear of the Island," agreed Old Stripe slowly, "and it would also get *them* clear of the Island, into the bargain! That's really clever of you, my dear Woo Owl!"

"It was your own suggestion," Woo Owl pointed out.

"Oh, was it? Then—then it's really clever of *me*, it doesn't make any difference."

Digger Mole looked at his Badgery friend with a wrinkle of mild confusion upon his velvet brow.

Everyone seemed to be getting Mixed. Or was it only he?

"That sounds very clever *indeed*," he said, wondering if it was, and hoping someone would tell him.

"*Eureka!*" cried Potter-the-Otter at that moment, and thumped the council-table so hard with his fist that small Mole leapt in his chair and bumped his knees underneath the edge of the table.

"I didn't quite catch that," said Woo, staring at Potter.

"Well, *I* did," mumbled Mole, rubbing his knees well again.

Potter was on his feet, and leaned over the table, looking excitedly at Woo, and then Stripe, and then Mole, as he talked.

"It's simple," he said. "I'll swim across to the Island, under water all the way, and——"

"You'd burst," said Mole. But no one heard him.

"——And I'll climb ashore, very quietly," Potter went on, lowering his voice impressively, "and I'll cut that ship adrift!"

Woo Owl frowned in feathery concentration. Old Stripe took his pipe out of his mouth, looked at it fondly, put it back, took a quiet puff or two, and said:

"Go on, Potter-folk."

"Then," he went on, "I'll swim back to the mainland, and we'll watch the galleon drifting downstream on the current. . . ."

"No!" said Woo. "We've already decided, my dear Cap'n Potter, that if they lose their ship, they'll

be marooned on your Island, and we shall be no
nearer evicting them!"

Digger Mole blinked. He had heard that word
before, and he still didn't know that it meant "turning
them out."

"But wait!" Potter told Woo Owl, "this is the point
of it! As soon as the galleon has got some way down
the river, we'll sling a rock or two across to the Island
to bring them out of my house, and *then* they'll see the
ship, drifting downwater without a soul on board
her!"

"Ha!" cried Old Stripe, waving his pipe. Then he
gave a frown, and added: "How will *that* help?"

Potter spread out his paws with a confident gesture.

"Don't you see, Old Stripe? They'll go after her, to
save her drifting right down to the brink of the Silver
Falls!"

Old Stripe's briar pipe dropped right out of his
mouth in surprise. Woo Owl raised his wings aloft
in excitement. Even Digger Mole could see the sense
of *that* idea.

"Wonderful!" cried Stripe, brushing the hot ash
from his knees where the fur was smouldering
gently.

"Terrifermous!" piped Mole gleefully.

"An admirable plan!" boomed Woo, and folded his
wings because of the draught they made. "They will
dive into the stream and swim after their ship, to stop
her from being wrecked by the Falls!"

"And once they're swimming after her," beamed
Potter-the-Otter, "we can cross to the Island, and

stand-by to defend its shores if they dare to come back!"

"Brilliant!" cried Stripe.

"Excellent!" hooted Woo, rising from his chair.

"Man the pumps!" shrilled Digger, catching himself on the knees again under the council-table. "Splice the mainbrace! Hurray for Potter-the-Otter!"

Woo Owl raised his wings for silence, and when it came, he said:

"Is it agreed, then?"

"Agreed!"

"Ay, it is!"

"Then, Gentlemen," said Woo, "let us go over our plan with all thoroughness."

"All right," said Potter, sitting down on his chair the wrong-way-round and folding his arms across the back of it, "while I'm swimming under water to the galleon, you folk can make a catapult of a couple of small saplings, and have a rock or two ready."

"Then we'll wait for you to swim back," nodded Stripe eagerly, "and as soon as the ship has got a little way downstream——"

"*Fire!*" cried Mole.

"Where?" hooted Woo Owl, leaping to his feet and gazing wildly round his sitting-room. Old Stripe and Potter had sprung from their chairs, and an ale-pot had gone spinning to the floor. The Badger's pipe had jerked from his mouth and now lay where it had fallen, after sliding the length of the council-table and leaving a trail of tobacco-ash in its wake.

Mole sat, very small, peering up at his friends.

84

"I—I *meant*," he whispered humbly, "I *meant* that *that* was when we must—er—*fire*—at the Island. . . ."

Woo Owl regarded his small velvet friend from beneath his heavily-feathered brows; and, after his beak had opened to utter something very fitting, it closed again, because he would not like to upset small Moles with angry words.

Old Stripe wrinkled his black-and-white brows, and went off with a sigh to the far end of the long council-table to fetch his favourite briar pipe. Potter-the-Otter sat down carefully, the wrong way round again, and said:

"*That*, as Digger Mole has pointed *out*, is when we shall fire on the Island. . . ."

From beneath the edge of the table, where he had slid in shame, inch by inch, Digger Mole's voice mumbled humbly:

"That's all I m-meant."

"Very well," said Woo Owl largely, now that this little point had been made crystal clear. "Now are we ready, Gentlemen?"

Potter looked to the windows, and studied the sky. The mist had cleared, and stars gleamed beyond the clustered beech-leaves all around. In the east, a faint radiance was seeping among the thin veils of cloud that topped the brink of the hills in that direction.

"We'll go now," he said, getting to his feet. "Dawn won't be long, and I must swim across before light comes."

He pushed his chair beneath the table, and Old Stripe rose, doing the same with his.

85

"Zero hour," said Woo dramatically, "has come!"

He stood up, shaking out his wings, and led the way to the door. Digger Mole wriggled round in his chair, and blinked slowly at his three friends as they made their way from the room.

"D-do you want Me to come?" he breathed in the smallest tone he possessed.

"Of course!" called Potter-the-Otter, "we shall want your help, Moley!"

Mole's chair tipped back and his legs twinkled from beneath the table and his whiskers sprang out straight and quivering in his excitement; and in an instant he was trotting eagerly across the room, to follow his three good friends. A small, humble, digging kind of ordinary, unremarkable Mole was wanted, upon an expedition most valorous and bold! Happily he followed, tumbling down the visiting ladder with his small pink feet a-going *slup-tup—dither-drrrpp— slither-sluther—brrpp-bop-BOMP*—all the way down the wooden rungs until he arrived at the ground (which was where the *BOMP* came in).

The starlight was pale as they crossed the sleepy glade, with Potter-the-Otter in the lead, a jack-knife in his paw. Woo Owl had found it for him in Owl's Beech, and it was used for peeling potaties in the ordinary way; but tonight was not an ordinary night. There were no potaties to be peeled, but the ropes of a foreign ship. . . .

There was no wind, no softest breeze, as they made along the woodland path towards the Wild River.

They reached the river's bank. The water ran by,

86

dreaming under the clearer spread of the sky, and
among the ripples ran the stars, set in their spangles
as in veils of drifting cloud.   No sound came from
anywhere on the waterway, nor from the Island, nor
from the great dark shape of the galleon that rode at
her mooring. No lamp shone from her deck or mast-
heads.

The river, the Isle and the ship were at slumber;
only the four Woodlanders were wakeful and alert.

Digger Mole was searching for some small rocks,
nearby the stream's bank. Old Stripe was seeking
two strong saplings that would make a catapult. Woo
Owl stood beside Potter, and spoke softly now:

"If you meet any trouble over there, old Potter,
give a shout, and I'll be with you as soon as I've
spread my wings, remember that."

"I shall remember," nodded Potter, and gripped the open jack-knife in his teeth.

"Be careful," murmured Woo, gazing across to the galleon.

"Good luck!" whispered Old Stripe, as Potter lowered himself into the stream without a splash.

"Take care," came Digger's voice, soft as a piping breath, "good luck, Potter-folk!"

For a moment Potter-the-Otter stood, waist-deep in the shallows near the bank, and waved one paw. Then, with a sudden flexing of his furry body that revealed his long experience of water and its ways, he dived, his tail flicking out behind his legs as a banner in the wind. The next moment he had gone.

To the east, the flush of first light was spreading in a tide of pale scarlet from the hills. On the Wild River, the ring of ripples Potter had left was now expanding, growing to a faint circle that, as it grew, became smoother, and fainter, and fainter yet, until the surface of the stream was still again, save for the gentle furrows of the current.

Somewhere in those darkling depths there swam the captain of the sunken *Dragonfly*; but no sign of him was there.

CHAPTER TEN

Ship Adrift!

There they sat, the pirates. Their shadows were on the wall behind them, cast by the flames of the fire they had built in the ancient hearth. The great black Otter was sprawled in his chair, with his thigh-booted legs outstretched; a wide belt was around his waist, and a kerchief at his throat; from the belt, a cutlass dangled in a leathern scabbard to the floor.

"Drink up!" he growled, raising his tankard in the candle-light. "To the health o' them woodland lubbers!"

The two Water-Rats raised their pots, with a grunt of merriment.

"To the lubbers o' the wood!" they answered, and drank deep of the nettle-ale.

"An' I'll say this of 'em," said their leader, wiping his mouth on his paw. "They know how to build a house, and how to make themselves snug!"

"And they know how to brew good ale!" quoth one of the Rats, banging his tankard upon his knee.

"Then what say," the Otter cried, "what say we stay on the Island here, to pass the rest of our days?"

"Agreed!"

"So we shall, Cap'n!"

"This can make our headquarters," he went on, stropping his gleaming black whiskers with a flourish of his paw, "and from here we can put out in our ship, to make a raid, and to bring back stores and booty!"

"*Hurray!*" cried the Rats, knowing full well that to disagree would be to bring their captain's fist upon their knavish heads.

"Stop that noise!" he roared, "or you'll deafen me with your brassy lungs, the pair of ye!"

They said not another word.

"Drink up, then!" he bellowed, and clapped a hand to his ear, for he deafened himself just as much. "Drink to ourselves—the Islanders!"

"The Islanders!" cried the two Rats; and one, leaning back a little too boisterously in his chair, tipped clean over backwards, kicking his captain under the chin as his foot swung upwards in the confusion.

"Strike me, would ye!" roared the Otter, as the Rat's ale-pot span into the air and crashed on his captain's head. The Otter staggered to his feet, with a lump on his chin and a bump on his head, and whipped out his cutlass, to swing it in a wicked circle while the Rats ducked for cover. The cutlass (whose blade was so blunt that it would scarce have cut a cheese) whirled against the tall candle on the shelf, and brought it down with a crack.

"Lights!" he roared, "*lights*, ye dogs o' thunder! Who put that candle out? Fetch a light, ye shiverin' bags o' skin an' bones!"

And he lunged out in the gloom, bringing down a chair, two ale-mugs and a three-legged stool before he fetched his head a hearty thwack against the mantelpiece and thudded to the floor.

A Rat struck tinder, and lit the fallen candle.

"Now I've got a headache," mumbled the Otter, and raised a paw to stroke the lump on his head. "Who set on me, hey?"

"You tripped," said a Rat, with a wink to his cuddy.

"You stumbled," the other one said.

"Tripped! Stumbled!" the captain grumbled, "well, get me to me bed!"

So they lifted him, the two Rats, and dumped him on to the couch that was in the corner of the room where a low bay window overlooked the stream.

"That's better," he said, "now fetch me something to ease this pesky lump!" He stroked his head most tenderly.

One Rat ran to the corner-cupboard, but there was nothing there but firewood. The other one ran to the kitchen, and brought back something in his paw.

"What's that?" roared the Otter, and winced at the sound of his own voice in his ears.

"'Tis a poultice, Cap'n! A fine bread-poultice!" And he clapped the cucumber-sandwich on top of the Otter's lump.

"Now take a turn outside, ye witless sons o' the sea, or we'll have them woodlanders here!"

They scuttled to the door, and left it wide as they went out. Moments later, when they heard the first snore from their captain, they crept back; and while one finished the flagon of cool nettle-ale, the other gently removed the Otter's 'bread-poultice' and munched it with enjoyment, for it was a fine fresh cucumber-sandwich, and was wasted upon such folk as the snoring captain. . . .

Before very long, the two Rats were lulled by the steady snores of the black Otter, and one sat down on the floor, his head lolling drowsily on his chest. The other curled up beneath the mantelpiece, near the warm, bright hearth. He was asleep within moments, and, as the melting wax of the candle dripped steadily from the shelf above him, and fell upon his furry chest, he dreamed that he was having an attack of heartburn; and his whiskers quivered fitfully as he slept.

There was peace at last, in the little stone-built house on Otter's Island, save for the trio of snores. The logs in the hearth burned low; and the candle guttered out, so that the Rat no longer dreamed of heartburn, but of munching endless sandwiches that appeared on his captain's head.

There was peace, at last. The Island's garrison dozed. Through the open window came the murmuring music of the stream; and soon, from the east, came the first pale prelude to the sun. But day had not yet come to the sleeping lands; and much was to happen before it was here.

A shape moved, at this moment, unseen. A shadow, as that of a great fish, glided beneath the surface of the stream; and, here and there, silver bubbles rose, to pop among the ripples. From the depths of the water this shadow came, moving in silence and out of sight towards the galleon moored to the Isle.

Beneath the dark hulk the shadow rose to the surface; and a fur-brown head lifted, breathing fast and blowing out a spray of water-mist. In the mouth was clenched a jack-knife.

Potter-the-Otter waited, with his head above the surface, until his eyes had grown used to the pale light, after the gloom of the depths, and could search the shore. His ears were pricked and alert; and for a moment he held his pent-up breath, to listen the better. There was no sound, and nothing he could see, save for the shadowed shore, the small house that he knew so well, and, looming above him, the shape of the foreigner's ship.

Rising in the water, he felt the touch of the sand beneath his feet, and waded slowly up the shore, keeping his eyes watchful for the enemy. None came. He grew more confident.

From the sides of the galleon, three ropes ran down to a single mooring-post. It was to the first rope that Potter crept, the jack-knife in his paw. Pausing a moment more, he listened, eyeing the house. No lamp was lit there, and no voices came.

The knife glinted as he raised it swiftly and slashed, slashed, slashed at the woven cords of the first rope; and the ends fell at his feet. The second was severed, and one end fell to the water, splashing there. Potter froze, thinking the slight sound might reach the ears of the foe.

It had not; or, if it had, they thought it was the beam-wash of the galleon as she swayed slightly to the current.

The third rope was cut, and, even as Potter gripped his knife between his teeth and waded into deeper water to dive beneath the surface, the foreign vessel moved.

The current swirled and the water eddied, whittling along her beams as she veered slowly, turning beam-on to the river's course. She moved a foot from the shore, and then a yard, and two, and more, until, with her canvas furled and no crew aboard, she felt the stronger tugging of the current in the mainwater, and she was away.

Potter saw nothing of this. He was rising, now, from the depths, and in a moment broke surface near the mainland bank. Only then did he turn his head, and saw the galleon making downwater, empty and adrift.

"Potter!" came a voice, "are you all right?"

"Come out, Potter-folk! Here's my paw!"

He waded to the alder-holts, and Old Stripe hauled him up.

"I'm right as a Robin," he told the Badger, and shook the water from his fur. Its beads glistened and glinted in the flush of light that now spread from the east.

"Can we rouse them?" piped Digger Mole.

Potter nodded.

"Get them out!" he said.

As the first sunbeam touched their faces, Woo Owl

95

stood by the catapult. Two saplings had been chosen, and between them was slung a length of rope, in the middle of which there had been made a cradle of thin cords, to hold the missiles.

"Load up!" said Woo Owl, judging the range.

Digger Mole heaved his rock into the cradle, and Old Stripe steadied it there.

"Aim for my kitchen window," Potter told them, gazing to the Island. "It's been cracked ever since Stripe hit it with a snowball, last Christmas, so I'll *have* to put a new one in if we finish it off!"

"Draw back," called Woo, whose keen sight was better than that of his friends.

Old Stripe and Digger Mole hauled on the rope, and the rock came back in its corded cradle, back and down, down and lower . . . lower . . .

"Ready!" grunted Stripe as the saplings strained and the rope quivered tautly under the tension.

"Then fire!" boomed Woo Owl.

Stripe and Mole let go. The saplings sprang. The rope snatched, jerking the rock—and the rock rose, curving across the wide waterway, to drop, hitting the reeds near the western shore, with a thud.

"Too short," said Woo, "again!"

Digger loaded the catapult a second time.

"Ready . . ." intoned Woo, judging the range again. Then—"Fire!"

The rock sang up, and fell with a crack, a yard from the wall of the house.

"Better," nodded Woo, "but still too short."

"Surely they heard it that time?" puffed Old

Stripe as he searched the ground for another missile.

"They'll be sound asleep, more like," grunted Potter, "or they'd have heard the wash of their ship as she drifted clear."

"If we don't rouse them soon," Mole declared, "they'll be too late to see it down the river!"

Potter-the-Otter cradled the third rock with a steady paw.

"We'll have 'em out with this one," he said grimly. "Ready, Old Stripe?"

"Ready, Cap'n Potter!"

They drew back, as Woo Owl stood beside the enormous catapult. The rock, half as big as Digger's own head, rested snugly in the cradle; and, as Stripe and Potter hauled back, Mole placed himself behind them, and grasped the belts of both.

"Back harder!" said Woo, determined that this time the rock should not fall short.

Stripe leaned back, digging his heels into the ground. Potter hauled strongly, with his feet against a tree-root. Digger Mole swung his whole weight from the belts of the other two.

"Harder!" said Woo, "harder!"

The saplings creaked under the final strain. The rope shivered and the knots became hard as iron. Stripe's heels were beginning to slide, and Potter's belt-buckle was near breaking, and Mole was a-going pink in the face as he swung with his short legs clear of the ground, when the order came:

"*Fire!*"

For a moment the rock appeared to hover, high above the stream; then it began its slow descent towards the Island house. Down . . . flashing across the reedy shore, down . . . singing over the mossy ground, down . . . shooting towards the wall of the house, where the kitchen window was.

It struck.

Even from here, the shatter of glass was loud; and Woo Owl could see the splinters shooting upwards, flashing in the sunbeams.

"Bravo!" he boomed, flapping his wings in glee.

"A bull's-eye!" piped up Mole, as he struggled to his feet. Old Stripe and Potter, who had tumbled over him backwards when the rope had been released, raised a sudden cheer.

Before their voices had faded on the morning air, a bellow reached their ears, from the distant Island shore.

"What in the name o' thundering sons o' Satan——" it began, and then there came a pause. The Black Otter could be seen clearly, standing outside the door of the house; and now he was joined by the two Rats as he gazed down the river. "Shivering shark-skins!" he roared, "*the galleon's gone!*"

"Then ye'd best go after her!" cried Potter, cupping his paws to his mouth. "See where she floats, you black-faced brigand."

The bewildered shout of the pirate came clearly across the water—"By all the saints and Davy Jones—she's drifting down to the falls! After her, you lazy sons o' lightning! After her, I say! A chest

o' golden sovereigns for the first to board my ship!"

And with a run he was diving into the river, the Rats on either side. Their arms threshed the water, sending it leaping and flashing in the morning sunshine, as they struck out with the current.

Potter-the-Otter watched their going.

"Scupper me sea-cocks," he breathed in amazement, "if we'd known there were only the three of them, we could have swum across and tackled them with our fists!"

"I thought they had a larger crew than that," nodded Old Stripe, gazing at the swimmers and then at the drifting vessel.

"Will they catch up with the ship?" asked Mole.

"They might," said Potter quietly, "and they might not. I hope they do."

"It might mean even more trouble, if they do," Woo pointed out.

Potter-the-Otter gazed to the drifting galleon, and in his eyes there was a strange light.

"Maybe," his friends heard him softly, "maybe it might, but I don't like to see a fine craft like her go to her doom over the Silver Falls, no I don't. . . ."

"A fine enough ship," said Stripe, "but a bad enough captain and crew."

"Well," said Woo, "we're rid of them now. Are you going to ask us over for breakfast, Cap'n Potter?"

Potter-the-Otter removed his gaze from the galleon and her swimming crew, and a beam came to his whiskery face.

"Breakfast!" he said cheerfully, *"b-b-breakfast*! I'd

clean forgotten *that*!" He leapt for the water's edge, and cupped his paws in front of him—"Who's for t-toast and m-marmalade?" he cried, and dived as clean as a fish. . . .

In went Mole with a plump old splash, and Old Stripe dived beside him. With a leisurely beat of his wings, Woo Owl took to the air, and flew slowly across the stream.

The Otter of Otter's Island was returning to his home, and with him went his three good friends, for toast and marmalade, and maybe a hot pot of tea.

CHAPTER ELEVEN

Honey-nut Toast

Potter-the-Otter stood outside his front door and then, as Woo Owl and Old Stripe and Digger Mole held back politely, the Otter entered his home.

"Welcome!" he said, as they followed him in, "though I don't know what we shall find. . . ."

"There'll be glass all over the kitchen floor," Woo reminded him, "we know that, for a start."

"And I'll wager my p-pantry isn't the s-same as when I l-l-left it," said Potter unhappily; but, when he trod carefully over the glass on the floor of the kitchen and opened the pantry door, he felt his spirits rise.

"Well, they've t-taken that m-mushroom pie," he told the others, "but they've had the d-decency to leave us enough for breakfast."

"Then I'll put the kettle on!" said Mole.

"All right," Potter nodded, "and I'll lay the table as soon as I've swept up this glass. Mind your feet there, Old Stripe!"

Digger Mole filled the big black kettle, and staggered with it to the hob. Then he took tinder and a flint-box, and arranged a heap of small faggots in the hearth, kindling them quickly by lying on his middle and puffing at them until he was pink with lackage of any more puff whatsoever. The flames leapt at last; and the kettle sat there, with that knowing expression all over its short black spout. It knew what was expected of it; but for a few minutes it was going to bide its time before it sang. Rome wasn't built in a day.

"Stripey!" called Potter as he began laying the table, "have a look in the pantry, and call out what there's there for us!"

While the Badger opened the large blue door, Woo Owl announced: "I'm going to fly down the river for a spell, to see what those brigands are doing!"

"Do!" nodded Potter, "and bring us the news! By the time you're back, there'll be toast and marmalade and a hot cup of tea for your thirst!"

Woo Owl licked the inside of his beak as he waddled to the door.

"Any more talk like that, old Potter, and I'm not sure I'll go at all. . . . "

But he went.

"Well," called Potter, laying a cup and saucer for each on the old oak table, "what have we got, Old Stripe?"

The Badger stood in the pantry doorway, surveying all the shelves.

"Two lettuces," he called out, "three loaves of honey-nut bread; a dish of cream; two boxes of short-bread; two dishes of chickory biscuits——"

"Two which?" enquired Mole, watching over his kettle.

"Two chisses of bickory discuits! I mean two bishes of dickory—oh, bother! Come and see for yourself, you ridicklemous Mole!"

"Busy," he said, and looked at his kettle again. At last it began a small little song; and Mole nodded comfortably.

The table was set. Four cups and four saucers, all of bright blue china; four wooden spoons, and a platter for each of them, and a space for spilling marmalade by mistake. Old Stripe busied himself between the table and the pantry, bringing dishes and bowls and pots and such, and the two large dishes of chickory-dockery, hickory-dickery biscuits.

"Ready!" called Mole, as the kettle sent a cloud of steam from its short black excited spout.

They sat them down, in the low-beamed room where the sunlight shone through the window that overlooked the stream. The murmur of the ripples drifted in, and on the ceiling was their bright reflection dappling and glimmering, shimmering as sunbright will-o'-the-wisps. The crockery clinked; the golden marmalade winked in the morning sun; steam rose from the teapot; and in a moment there came the delightful aroma of toast, as the slices of honey-nut bread that Mole had propped in the hearth began browning for the feast.

"Breakfast . . ." murmured Potter, sipping his tea and savouring the word. "There's nothing that's quite like breakfast, you know, no matter what they say. . . ."

"There nothing is," agreed Old Stripe, and helped Digger Mole with the toast.

Potter-the-Otter sat contented, and slowly he shook his head.

"There's nothing *quite*," he said.

For he was back in the stone-built house, the well-loved, friendly old house that some time and many a year ago had been built by one of his own forbears, an Otter like himself. For a few hours, it had been lost to the river bandit; but it would never be lost again. Never, thought Potter, again—or his name was not Potter-the-Otter, of Otter's Island, Deep Wood.

"Hot toast!" said Mole, "piping hot toast!" And he stacked it upon a dish, honey and nutty and golden-brown. Then he and the Badger sat down.

Woo Owl beat his slow wings, down along the course of the winding river. The Wood was decked in bright new morning-green; the water beneath him winked and sparkled, and his slow shadow moved along the bank, where brook-lime was opening its purple blooms to the warmth.

A quarter-mile or more from Silver Falls, he sighted the ship; she seemed to be drifting on, her sails still furled. As the Owl swooped low above the water, he saw three tiny figures on board; and in a moment he heard the voice of the Black Otter, driving his crew of Rats.

"Get those oars moving! Rig them sails, will you, you lazy louts! Keep over with that helm—*and get that canvas spread!*"

As Woo dived low over the decks, he saw the confusion that had come to the pirate and his crew— for they could not man the oars, rig the sails and mind the helm, all at the same time. They were so frantic with the work that they did not notice him. But he had seen all he needed. The galleon was drifting onwards for the falls; and no matter what those scoundrels might do now, they could not save her. At the last moment they would have to leap overboard and swim to the bank and safety, to watch their ship go down over the rocky brink.

"That," murmured Woo to himself as he wheeled in the air, "is going to be a pity; but it's not more than those brigands deserve. . . ."

He set his course upstream, and winged swiftly back to Otter's Island. As he neared the small green mound of land that was ringed with its sandy shores, he heard singing, and the strains of some musical instrument. Digger Mole had found a concertina that the pirates had left behind.

> ". . . *Oh, who'd be a Pirate,*
> *Who'd be a Bandit,*
> *Who'd be a Robber bold?*
> *Who wants Treasure, who wants Trove?*
> *Who wants to Smuggle in a Smuggler's Cove?*
> *Who wants a Ship full o' Gold?*
>
> *O-o-h, I'd rather have a Home*
> *Than sail the Foam,*
> *Rather have a Pot full o' Tea!*

There's nothing like a Hearth
And a trim Front-path,
So this is the Place—
    —f-o-o-r—
        —M-e-e-e!"

Woo Owl stood in the doorway and blinked at his noisy friends.

"Hello, Woo!" cried Digger Mole, in the middle of his hornpipe on the three-legged stool.

"Come and sit down!" beamed Potter, "there's toast keeping hot, and tea in the pot!"

"What's the morning like?" asked Old Stripe, putting down the concertina.

"It's a better morning for us-folk," declared Woo

as he sat down at the breakfast-table, "than it is for those pirates, I can assure you."

Potter glanced at him as he brought the kettle over. "You saw the ship, Woo?"

"I did. They've climbed aboard her, but if you ask me they'll be too late to do anything."

Old Stripe leaned against the window-sill, filling his black briar pipe. Digger Mole slid the butter-dish and the pot of marmalade along the table so that Woo could help himself. But it was Potter who was the most interested in what the Owl was telling them.

"How far is the galleon from the Falls, then?"

"When I left it, they were rounding the last curve of the river, between Stricken Oak and the fork, but it was still drifting fast."

"Going to shoot the rapids, is she," murmured Potter, and stared from the window to where the ripples winked and flashed between the banks of the stream.

"Well," said Mole, "they did *ask* for trouble, didn't they? They sent our *Dragonfly* to the bottom without thinking twice about it."

Potter-the-Otter nodded slowly.

"I know that, Digger Mole, I know that, and it's just what they deserve, I grant you. All the same, that galleon is one o' the finest craft I've ever set eyes on; and there's no true river-folk or sea-folk as likes to think of a good ship breaking her heart on the rocks for the want of a bit of help . . ."

Old Stripe looked at his friend through the smoke of his pipe, and his voice was quiet.

"I can see it your way, Cap'n Potter. Fine two-master, she is, and not long out of the builder's yard, aren't I right?"

"You're right enough, Old Stripe, she wasn't built very long ago, and soon those stout beams o' hers are going to break against . . ." he did not finish, but looked in silence at the bright water that hurried past the Island shores.

Digger Mole stropped a whisker, idly with an idle paw. He, too, knew what thoughts were running through the Otter's mind.

Woo Owl finished his cup of tea, and gazed at the table in front of him. There was more toast, and marmalade a-plenty, and a half-a-potful of tea; but somehow he didn't want any more breakfast. Potter's restlessness was felt by all in the quiet, sunny room.

Old Stripe spoke.

"Potter, you're master of the Wild River, so far as it's nearby the Wood, and I think you should speak your mind."

"Ay," murmured Digger Mole.

"You must," nodded Woo Owl slowly.

For a moment the Otter made no reply to this. Then, as he watched the ripples winking out there, and thought of that mighty cascade of water that plunged from the edge of the Silver Falls to the river's bed below, his eyes were lit, and his answer came suddenly——

"I—I'd like to save that ship!"

Digger Mole stopped stropping of his bright-and-shiny whiskers; and Woo Owl got up from his chair; and Old Stripe turned to the door:

"Then so we shall!" he cried.

Woo Owl waddled after him: "We'll have to be quick about it, too!" he boomed urgently, "or we'll be too late."

Digger Mole grabbed the concertina and followed them outside—for you never could tell when such a thing might come in handy, wherever you happened to be.

CHAPTER TWELVE

Captain of the Galleon

Old Stripe gulped for breath as he raced along the path by the river bank, making for the Silver Falls. Woo Owl was ahead of the others, beating his wings every few moments to keep himself going without too much effort from his feet. Potter-the-Otter kept up with the Badger; and behind them ran Mole, just as puffed but a little slower, because of the trouble his legs gave him. But, if they were shorter than most folks', they moved more quickly, and that made up for things.

They ran past Fallen Elm, where Skip Squirrel had his house. They went down into Copperbeech Spinney, taking a short cut, and climbed the hillock where the wild strawberries grew. They tripped upon tree-roots and bumped their elbows where the saplings grew thickly along the path; they brushed their heads against twigs and leaves as they darted through Brambly Way.

"What's the hurry?" called Timber Jim, the Squirrel who lived near the path.

"Galleon in trouble!" panted small Digger Mole as he followed the others along.

"Gallon of bubbles?" murmured Timber Jim, gazing after them and scratching his head in surprise. "What *sort* of bubbles, I wonder," he pondered, "a gallon of what *sort* of such?"

But Potter and Woo and Mole and Stripe were away down the path.

"What's the haste?" cried a Jackdaw, looking down from his lofty doorstep.

"Can't stop!" piped Mole, and followed the others, down to the Wild River's bank.

"Well, this is a very hot morning," frowned the Jackdaw, staring after them in bewilderment, "this is a *very* hot morning, for not *stopping*," he said.

But it seemed they didn't know, for they went on running, into the leafy shade of Tangle Glen, out into the sunlit glades, down along the riverbank until, at last, they heard the muted murmur of the falls.

The bright river lay before them, a great expanse of sun-reflection between the wide green banks; and there, in midwater, stood the pirate's galleon, tall and graceful above her own reflection.

"She's lost!" cried Potter, halting by the water's edge, "we're—too late!"

Old Stripe and Digger Mole and Woo Owl came to a stop, struggling to gather their breath. Potter stood helpless, his paws clenched, watching that great ship as she drifted over the last few yards to the brink of the Silver Falls.

They heard the captain's voice; but he was shouting in vain:

"Pull on them oars, ye lazy louts! Pull, pull, *pull*, will ye, pull on them oars, ye lubbers!"

The oars—great oars they were, poking through the rowlock-holes on the starboard beam—flexed and shivered as the two Rats heaved, heaved, heaved until their arms must surely crack!

The captain was working, but he worked in vain. With his feet astride he stood to the helm and spun it with all his might, to bring it back slowly, to spin it again.

"Heave," he bellowed to his crew, "heave there, will ye, heave—heave—*heave*!"

The crew strained their muscles, but they strained their muscles in vain.

"She's done," said Potter.

"Pull!" roared the Black Otter, "pull, ye limbs o' thunder, will ye, heave—heave—*heave!*"

"She's lost," said Potter-the-Otter, his voice soft and his brown eyes wide.

Woo stood motionless, knowing that even if he flew across to the struggling ship, there was nothing he might do to save her now; for she was drifting faster, moment upon moment, as the great current near the falls took her with its rising strength and dragged, tugged, pulled her to the brink. Fifty oars could not have overcome that mighty drift; and there were but two of them.

Old Stripe looked on with a furrowed brow, knowing what this sight must mean to his friend Potter, and knowing also that even if they all dived to the river and swam across, there was nothing they could do.

Digger Mole stood panting, his concertina hanging from his paw. If two Otters, two Rats, a Badger and an Owl could think of no way to save the vessel, he was sure, was small Digger Mole, that a small Digging Mole could not.

Now the pirate had ceased his shouting, and the helm swung no more in his paws. He was gazing ahead, over the bows of his ship, to the dizzy brink of the river that was nearing swiftly, swiftly as he watched.

"Drop those oars!" he ordered; and they splashed, idle in the current. "Jump!" he called, "jump, and swim for your lives!"

The two Rats leapt from their seats, and clambered

to the deck. But the Black Otter remained at the helm, staring over the bows. The Rats hesitated, waiting for him to join them. He made no move to the side.

"Thank ye for what ye tried to do," he called, "it was no fault o' yours that ye failed—now jump, will ye! Swim, ye devils, swim for the bank, I say!"

The falls roared, as loud as his shout; the current swirled, drawing the ship to the brink.

"Not without, you, Cap'n!" the Rats cried out.

"Jump, I command! Obey my orders and jump, ye rogues!"

The falls thundered, drowning his voice. The Rats remained where they were. The pirate stood by his helm.

On the bank, Potter had begun running to the cliff of sandstone that flanked the falls; and his friends went with him.

"There won't be much chance to save them!" he called; but they ran with him to the cliff. They would scramble down the face of it, down to the valley-bed far below, where the galleon would smash to the bottom; but what they could do then was doubtful indeed.

With a last glance at the vessel, whose bows were even now poised at the brink of water, Potter halted and swung himself over the edge, his feet feeling for support on the lower ledges and stumps of sprouting bush. Woo Owl beat his wings and rose, to glide down over the cliff. Old Stripe followed Potter, and last came Digger Mole.

So that it was Digger Mole who was first aware of the miracle.

115

Above the mighty thunder of the waters, he heard another sound, and turned his head. The sound was of timber grating upon rock; and, as he stared to where the galleon reared at the brink, he saw the length and breadth of her shudder; and the masts shook, shivering as saplings to a wind.

"Stripe!" came Mole's shrill cry above the roaring of the falls. "Potter! *Come back!*"

Woo Owl, hearing that reedy cry from where he glided beyond the face of the cliff, drove his wings and rose, lifting into the sunshine and wheeling back to the path by the river's bank.

"Come back, Stripe—Potter, come back!"

Woo landed with a rush, and small Mole leapt in his velvet, for he had thought his winged friend was too far down the cliff to hear his call.

"Look, Woo Owl—*look there!*"

As Stripe came clambering back over the edge of the sandstone cliff, and Potter-the-Otter followed, Mole raised a pink and trembling paw; and Woo Owl looked, and saw.

As though held back from that dizzy brink of water by magic, invisible cords, the galleon rode, motionless, drifting no more. The Black Otter was staring over the starboad side, together with his crew.

"What—what's happened?" called Mole, as Potter came running up. For a moment the river-folk stared, shielding his eyes with a paw. Then a great sigh of relief welled up in his furry chest.

"She's caught by the keel on the rocks!" he told his friends.

"Are there rocks, there at the brink?" gasped Old Stripe.

"Ay," nodded Potter, who knew every inch of the river's bed, "and a smaller craft would have cleared 'em easily—but with a ship of that size and a keel as deep as hers, they've got her with their teeth!"

"B-but it's a miracle!" cried Mole, gazing at the ship.

"Ay," said Potter, "a miracle it is, Digger Mole."

He stared at the grounded galleon, and only Mole heard his voice above the sound of the falls as he went on quietly:

"Now ye know why sometimes a captain'll refuse to abandon his ship, no matter what peril she's in. They just won't believe that their own ship can ever go to the bottom, and that's why they stay at the helm, sure that the miracle will come . . ."

Digger Mole's small bright eyes were wide.

"And it has!" he said, "the miracle has!"

"This time," nodded the river-folk, "ay, this time it has. That captain's prayer came true enough, so he can't be as black as he looks." He cupped his paws of a sudden, and his voice rang across the swirling water: "Ahoy there, galleon! A-hoy, Cap'n Pirate!"

"They're baling water out," said Old Stripe, "look!"

"A-hoy the galleon!" shouted Potter again. This time a reply came, as the Black Otter peered from the stern of his stricken ship, where the Rats were baling water.

"What do ye want, Woodlander?"

"Throw me a line!" Potter cried.

The pirate stared, then threw up his arms before he returned to help his crew bale out water that was entering the holds from a shattered plank or two. Potter-the-Otter turned to Woo Owl:

"Will you fly to the ship?" he asked. Woo nodded. "I will, Cap'n Potter!"

"Good! Find out if she's taking in much water. I think the rocks have split her beams below, and she may be settling. And bring back a line with one end fast to the galleon!"

"A line, Potter?"

"Ay—I'm going aboard, whether that scoundrel likes it or no!"

Woo Owl nodded, and rose from the bank, to glide across the water and then dive, swooping to the deck of the vessel. He landed with a thud, and the pirate wheeled about, a baling-pitcher raised in his paw.

"Off my ship, you Woodlander! Ye hear?"

"Kindly desist," shouted Woo crossly, above the noise of the falls, "and be good enough to listen. The Otter of Otter's Island wishes to come aboard!"

"Does he now, friend Owl? An' what if we're a mite too busy to receive visitors, hey?"

Woo peered at the two Rats, who were baling out the water that was gurgling in, as fast as they could go.

"You'll be a mite busier still," he told the pirate, "if you don't soon have some help!" And he waddled sideways a pace, to save his feet from getting wet.

"An' why should the Otter help *me*?" shouted the pirate. "Didn't I sink his own ship, on the main-water?"

"There's no time to argue!" retorted Woo warmly. "If you don't want to go down the falls, give me a line, for I'm not stopping here all the day, I assure you!"

The Black Otter eyed him strangely, trying to puzzle this out. Then, as he saw the two Rats were losing their fight against the inrushing waters, he shrugged, and strode over to a stanchion, tying a line to it. Clumping back in his heavy sea-boots, he gave the other end to Woo.

"Well," he shouted, "here's your line! I'll pay it out as ye go!"

Without another word, Woo gripped the cord securely in his toes. Out across the swirling water he flew, with the line trailing as the captain paid it away as fast as his paws could move.

"Bravo, Woo Owl!" piped Digger Mole, beside himself with excitement.

"Good work!" cried Potter, and seized the line as Woo landed on the mossy bank. Running it round a nearby willow, he lashed it tight.

"Take care," Woo told him, "that current is like a gale o' water near the brink!"

"I'll be all right with the rope," Potter answered him.

"What if it breaks?" asked Digger.

"If it breaks," said Woo, "I'll try to fly him clear!"

"I don't like it at *all*," said Old Stripe uneasily.

But Potter was lowering himself into the stream, one arm hooked over the landline.

"I'll be back before long!" he called; and in a

moment he was fighting the current, swimming with his legs and following the rope, paw over paw.

As he reached the side of the listing galleon, the pirate leaned over, holding out his paw.

"Take hold, Woodlander!" he called, and the next moment was hauling Potter from the water.

"Cap'n Pirate," said he, as he shook his fur dry, "we want to save your ship!"

"What can you do? My sailors are baling out as fast as they can, but the water's winning. There's a split in the planks as wide as your own shoulders—we'll not stop that breach if fifty of us bale all the day!"

"We'll save this vessel," replied Potter, "but we'll do it on our own terms!"

"And what are they, Islander?"

"That everyone on board takes orders from me!"

"What? You take command o' my own ship?"

"Ay, until she's saved—then you can have her back!"

The pirate eyed him, undecided.

"But what in Davy Jones can ye do?" he asked.

"Save precious time—by not wasting any more with talking! D'you accept my offer, or no?"

The Black Otter laughed grimly.

"Ay, for what it's worth!"

"You accept?"

"I do, Woodlander!"

Potter thrust out his paw.

"Good! We'll shake on that!"

And the Black Otter and the brown, the pirate and

the Islander, shook their paws solemnly on board the pirate galleon. Stricken though she lay, with her beams rent upon the teeth of the rocky brink above the falls, she had, now, a new captain, until such time as she was saved.

CHAPTER THIRTEEN

Planking, Pegs and Pitch

"First thing we must do," said Cap'n Potter, as he inspected the breach in the planks, "is to fill that hole, and stop any more water coming in."

The Black Otter shrugged helplessly.

"Why, Cap'n," he growled, "we can't mend the planks before we lift the ship from the rocks—for they're pokin' through the hole—look there. An' if we lift the ship, she'll be clear o' the rocks, and then there's nothing to stop her drifting down the falls!"

"I know," nodded Potter, rubbing his chin and pondering the matter deeply, "but we can try it with a rope to the shore on either side."

"A rope? How mean ye?"

"Sling a stout line from the starboard beam, I mean, across the river to the willow there. Sling another from the port beam, across the river to that alder-stump on the other bank. Then throw out your cargo—jettison everything on board to lighten the ship. When she rises in the water, and clears the rocks, those ropes will hold her back from the brink while we mend the breach in her planks."

The Black Otter listened carefully, frowning and

nodding as the captain of his vessel outlined his plan.

"Ay," he said at last, "but what if the ropes don't hold? She's a great craft, ye know."

"Then," said Potter grimly, "we'll use four ropes—we'll sling six across, six as thick as your fist!"

Again the pirate nodded.

"And how to mend the planks, Cap'n? That breach is a yard wide, and ten yards long!"

"I've got new planks enough, in the boat-shed on my Island, and pitch, too, and pegs and mallets—we'll fix that breach right enough, given a bit of time."

The pirate stroked his chin, and nodded again.

"Shiver me timbers, Cap'n, but 'tis worth a try, I'll say that for your plan!"

"Good! Then keep your crew baling. I'll send for some of my friends to help them—have you any more pitchers for the work?"

"Plenty, ay plenty!"

"Then keep those Water-Rats baling until the others come!"

As Potter turned away, and climbed the wooden ladder to the deck above, he heard the pirate's orders roaring out anew:

"Bale there, keep that water down, will ye! Bale, me lads, bale, bale, *bale!*"

Potter found Woo Owl, waiting on deck.

"Fly to the bank, Woo Owl, and ask Stripe and Digger to come across by the landline! Stand-by to get them clear if the rope breaks—and tell them to cross one at a time!"

As Woo nodded swiftly and beat his wings, Potter ran down to the hold in the stern and, with the bandit, snatched up a pitcher, until the four of them were baling, scooping, slinging the water over the stern, splashing it back as it gurgled in through the breach in the splintered planks.

Almost before Potter had begun work with his pitcher, Old Stripe had received Woo's message on the river's bank, and now lowered himself into the water, the landline in one paw. Clinging to it, kicking his legs out against the tugging of the current, he made his slow and difficult way from the bank to the galleon's side; and when he was hauling himself up, Digger Mole dropped from the bank, and began his journey across. Woo Owl wheeled above him, his wings spread wide as he circled within a few yards of the small and bobbing figure. If the rope snapped, or Digger lost his grip, Woo would swoop in the same instant, to fly him clear of the brink, drag though the current might. But the rope did not break, woven as it was by pirates' paws and strong in every fibre of its length.

As Old Stripe came scampering down the ladder to the hold, Potter gave him his pitcher, and went up on deck, to haul Digger safely over the ship's side. Woo Owl came down, furling his wings.

"Help them bale, will ye, Digger Mole?"

Digger Mole vanished down the ladder with his pink feet slipping and dithering and a-going *drrp— brrrp—bomp*! into the hold—for small Mole had never been asked to save a pirate galleon, not ever before in his life; and he was more excited than he had been since Old Stripe had caught his whiskers afire last Pancake Tuesday when he was lighting his pipe.

"Woo," said Potter quickly when Mole had gone down to join the baling-crew, "will you fly again for me?"

"Swim," said Woo, "if needs be!"

"Good! There's no call for swimming, but fly to the Island, and fetch the spare planks down here from my boat-shed—there are about a dozen, of beech-wood. Bring the keg of pitch you'll find near the door. and a score or so of pegs, and four mallets—and as much rope as you can find on the Island!"

Woo shook his wings out in a getting-ready manner.

"Twelve planks," he boomed against the sound of the waterfall, "keg of pitch, score or so of pegs, four mallets, and all the rope that's there. Is that all?"

"No," said Potter. "When you've made a raft of the planks, you can put the keg and other stuff on board, and set it floating down. We'll be on the look-out for it, and we'll fetch it in from the water as it comes by."

Woo nodded, thinking this was all; but no . . .

"As soon as ye've set the raft drifting," Potter went on quickly, "fly to some of our neighbours, those who'll be likely to have a bit of rope in their store-rooms—Skip Squirrel at Fallen Elm, Mole-the-Miller up on the Hill—and see how much Old Mr. Nibble can let you have from Deep Wood Store!"

"Is *that* all?" asked Woo, stretching his wings.

"I think so. How long will it take you?"

"No longer than I can help!" declared the Owl;

and he lifted from the deck a moment later, wheeling in the air and setting a southward course, upstream to Otter's Island. Before he was out of sight, Cap'n Potter was down in the hold, helping the others bale.

Woo Owl flew swiftly, and below him his shadow followed, rippling along the mossy bank of the river, passing tree and shrub, creek and pool, swimming over the sunlit land and water until it swerved from the mainland to the shore of the Isle, as Woo came down, swooping for the boat-shed.

There were the planks, more than twelve, stacked against a wall. There was the keg of pitch, standing near the door. With two lengths of rope he lashed the planks loosely, dragging them one by one to the water's edge and making a raft of them. Then the little fat keg was rolled down the sand, and stood in the centre of the raft. Pegs were brought from the boat-house cupboard, and mallets from the shelf. Last of all, Woo searched out every length of rope he could discover, in the boat-shed, the summer-house, and the store-room of Potter's dwelling.

The raft weighed fairish by the time it was loaded up; and Woo hauled on the ends of the ropes, wading into the stream. It did not budge. He brought a stout boat-hook from the shed, and levered against the planks. But the pole ploughed up the sand; and the raft remained where it was.

"Oh, pish!" declared Woo crossly, and heaved and hauled and levered and dragged and puffed and panted and cussed, most breathless and cussy, he did.

"Oh, tosh and—and *buttle!*" he announced; but the

127

raft stayed where it was. Finally, when he had run out of cuss, he sat down on the sand, leaned back on his wings, put his large feet against the raft's edge, and pushed—and pushed—and pushed as he never had before in all his days, until, at last, something had to budge; and it was not Woo Owl (for it was he who refused).

The water lapped over the raft, swamping it, as it slid into the stream; and with a final push, the Owl drove it off the shore, watching it until the main current took it, and started it upon its drifting journey to the galleon by the falls.

Leaving the deep imprint of his feathery nethers in the sand, Woo waddled breathlessly up the beach, and mopped his brow with a sandy wing.

"So there," he murmured in mild triumph, his task completed. "It's the cussing that does it. A few good pishes and a tosh and a buttle, and a folk can do almost anything."

He stretched his wings, beat them slowly, and rose into the sunlit air, veering downstream to overtake the raft and fly onwards, back to the galleon. As he neared the listing vessel, he went into a steep dive and passed above the stern with no more than a yard to spare.

"*Raft afloat!*" he called down; and Potter heard the booming voice and looked up, waving an answer. Woo turned his wings, vaning the feathers, and wheeled, flying into the trees beyond the bank, to call upon Skip Squirrel of Fallen Elm, Mole-the-Miller upon Heather Hill, and Old Nibble of the Store.

From Fallen Elm he first flew back to the ship, with two coils of rope gripped in his feet. Cap'n Potter waved him down to the bows, where he dropped the rope and landed with a thump.

"That's from Skip Squirrel!" he puffed.

"We shall need more!" answered Potter, judging the length of the coils.

"I'm going to the Store, next," nodded Woo, "but I sighted the raft as I came down—it's coming round the bend!"

"Can ye get a rope to it?"

"I can, Cap'n!"

So while Potter-the-Otter lashed a cord to a stanchion in the bows, Woo took off again, the other end gripped in his toes. Hovering, he waited; and as the raft came drifting downstream he flew lower, landing upon the bobbing planks, to lash his rope to one of those that bound them.

"Good work!" shouted Potter, and waved his paw.

Through the long morning the toil went on without a pause. The Black Otter baled with his crew, Old Stripe and Digger Mole. Cap'n Potter collected the planks and the pitch, the mallets and the pegs, and made them ready for the task that was soon to come. The rope he sorted out, doubling coils and joining them, making the knots as fast and as strong as only his paws knew how.

By noon, Cap'n Potter was ready to put the first part of his courageous plan into action.

"Woo Owl," he called, "have you had a rest?"

"No!" replied Woo, "but I'm ready!"

"There's not much more to do," Potter told him, "and then we can all stop work for a while before we begin again!" He looked at the two ropes that lay coiled in the bows. One end of each of these great hempen cables was tied to a stanchion, the other end lay free.

"Take one o' these, will you, Woo Owl, and fly it to the bank over there—there where the alder-stump stands!"

"And lash it round?" asked Woo, gripping the rope's end between his weary toes.

"Ay," nodded his captain, "lash it well, for it's to take half the strain of the galleon when she clears those rocks below!"

As the Owl rose and flew low across the water, with his rope trailing after him, Potter-the-Otter took the free end of the second, and lowered himself over the other side of the vessel. Paw over paw, he crossed the swirling water to the bank, opposite that where Woo was lashing his rope to the alder-stump and made the cable fast round the sun-warm bole of a willow.

When he was back on board the galleon, Woo was waiting for him.

"What now, Cap'n?" he puffed, hoping there would be a moment's rest before he began again.

"There's nothing more you can do, Woo Owl!"

Woo Owl's eyes opened wide, and he flopped down on to the deck with a puff of sheer relief. Potter was running down the ladder to the hold in the stern of the ship.

"Cap'n Pirate!"

"Ay, Cap'n Woodlander?"

"We've got ropes out, reaching to the bank on either side! They'll hold the ship well enough, once she lifts and clears the rocks! Now you must jettison your cargo!"

The Black Bandit poked his head from the hatchway, and saw the two great cables that stretched from the starboard bow to the willow, and from the port bow to the alder-stump on the other bank.

"If one o' them cables breaks, Cap'n Woodlander, the ship'll drift over the falls—and we with her! Ye know that?"

"I made those ropes with my own paws," Potter told him briefly, "and they're lashed with knots that'll tighten to the strain! Get your cargo overboard, those are my orders!"

The pirate eyed him for a moment, then, perhaps

remembering his bargain, he raised his voice to his crew:

"Stop baling, there, and jettison cargo!"

The two Rats flung their pitchers down, wiping their brows with their tails.

"Jettison——"

"Cargo?" they gasped, knowing nothing of Cap'n Potter's plan.

"Every stick and box!" roared the Black Bandit, and he made a start himself, heaving a keg to the side and slinging it clear. The two Otters and the two Water-Rats bent to their work. They dragged timber from the decks, and sent it overboard; they hauled stores from the holds—chests and boxes, sea-bags and movable lockers—and tumbled them over the side; they cleared the holds, the decks, the living-quarters and the captain's bridge, moving from the stern to the prow and slinging into the water everything that was not fixed to the ship.

Before all was done, Potter went below, and called to his two friends:

"Stop baling, Stripey! Throw down that pitcher, Digger Mole!"

"It's still coming in fast!" cried the Badger, and Mole waded knee-deep in the hold.

"Let it do its worst!" Potter told them. "We're jettisoning cargo, and the ship's rising in the water, fast. I want you folk to stand-by to help me when we clear the rocks!"

"I'm ready!" said Stripe, throwing down his baler.

"Ready and waiting!" said Mole.

"She's rising!" called the Black Otter from the deck.

"Ay, she's clearing the rocks!" cried Potter.

The waters swirled angrily now, and Digger Mole was clinging to a beam. The ship had been lifting inch by inch, as the weight of the cargo had gone overboard. Moment by moment the stricken vessel had been growing lighter; and, as her shattered planks had lifted from the jagged teeth of the rocks, the water had found more room to enter the breach.

"Be ready!" shouted Potter, and heaved the first of the new planks into the swirling water, forcing it into the gap torn by the rocks. Old Stripe was ready with pegs and mallet; and as the new planks went in, he hammered as fast as he could go, banging and splashing, working half under-water while Digger Mole slapped pawfuls of pitch from the keg, pressing it home with a mallet.

The pirate and his crew came thudding down the ladder.

"All cargo overboard, Cap'n Woodlander!"

For an instant Potter paused, lifting his head. This was their most perilous moment, for, with the cargo gone, the ship had risen from the teeth of the rocks, and was riding the water, free—free except for those two great cables that ran to either bank.

"Then—then the ropes are holding us!" he cried, and bent to his planking again, shouting over his shoulder: "get to work with the pitchers, Cap'n Pirate, and bale while we mend!"

They were about to see the result of their unceasing toil, for, as the breach was slowly filled, the water was slowly baled out: until at last no more came in. Potter and Stripe, Digger and Woo forced down the planks into the narrowing gap, pegged and hammered them fast, and pitched them well.

Before the sun rose to its noon zenith in the clear sky, the inrush of water had dwindled to a steady leak; the leak to a trickle; and now even the trickle had ceased.

When the last new plank was laid, and pegged, and pitched, Potter-the-Otter straightened up, and seized another pitcher, throwing out the water that remained, with the help of the others. Old Stripe flung down his mallet, and baled. Digger Mole looked round for a pitcher; but there were now no more to spare.

"Is that keg empty of pitch?" panted the Black Otter, seeing Mole searching in vain.

"Ay, for I've used every bit!"

"Then take my pitcher, friend Mole, and throw me over that keg!"

And as Mole began a-baling, the bandit grasped the fat little keg in his two muscular paws, and slung more water with it than four full pitchers could hold.

The flood grew lower. The balers worked, scooping, flinging, scooping, tossing out the water over the side of the ship, where it flashed in the sunlight, sending a mist of rainbows before it fell to the current that was swirling over the falls.

At last Cap'n Potter straightened his back, and threw his pitcher down. The others stopped work, their chests heaving and their muscles aching fit to catch afire.

The Black Otter dropped his fat round keg, and drew a paw across his brow. The rocks had been cleared. The great breach that they had shattered into the planking was repaired, and well repaired. The pirate ship rode free, on the rush of water by the rapids' brink, held safe by the two great ropes that reached to willow-bole and alder-stump, one upon each bank.

There was a strange light in the eyes of the Black Otter as he stood there, gathering his breath. His voice came hoarsely from his throat, and there was wonderment in its tone as he turned to Potter-the-Otter.

"Cap'n Islander, she's safe—my ship's safe! But by all the barnacles on her hull, I never thought ye'd do it! No, I never believed!"

Cap'n Potter put his paws on his hips, and looked at the soaking planks.

"She's safe, ay," he said, "but we've still to get her upstream, away from this current by the falls. We'll take a rest for a while, before we start work again."

They went on deck, where the sunshine was blazing down; and they lay them there, flat on their backs, to let the sun's beams dry their fur while their muscles rested and their strength came slowly back.

CHAPTER FOURTEEN

Home to the Island

As the sun moved down from its zenith, and began the long journey through the afternoon to the horizon in the west, a gallant spectacle was seen upon the Wild River.

The pirate craft still rode the water, within yards of the brink of the falls, held back by the two great ropes from either bank. But since noon, Woo Owl had been flying through the Wood, knocking at doors, calling down chimneys, tapping at windows, visiting those folk who were in their gardens or cutting the lawn or just sitting and a-doing nothing in the sun.

"Grey Squirrel, we need your help at the Silver Falls, will you come?"

Woo had flown on, on to Meadow Rise:

"Edward Hedgehog, will you come and help us save a ship, at the edge of the waterfall?"

His wings had beat again, and he had swooped:

"Badger Brown, can you come to the falls? We need your help—will you come?"

And onwards, through the Wood, to the dwellings in the glades and thickets, copses and tall tree-tops, with the urgent message, the call for help.

Woo Owl had come back; but long before he had finished his vital errand among the trees, many a folk had come down to the river bank—Squirrel and Hedgehog and Badger Brown, and many another besides; so that, as the sun came down from the top of the sky, and the afternoon began, a gallant spectacle was seen near the Silver Falls.

The vessel rode, high on the water; the two hempen cables tautened, jerking, and slackened, whipping, as the current tugged at the ship. On board was Cap'n Potter, the Black Bandit, the two Rats, Stripe, Digger Mole, and Woo Owl. They waited another moment.

Along the banks, where stood the willow on the one shore and the alder-stump on the other, were ranged these many folk—a score of them or thirty or even more, lined up along the ends of the two great ropes, from the water's edge to the timbers where they were lashed.

The second part of Potter's plan was about to be put to the test. Before the vessel was safe, she must be moved from that tugging current that slipped beneath her keel and past her beams, seeking to draw her over the brink, to her doom in the valley-bed beneath. There was no wind for her sails; there were but half a dozen oars. Six oars could never drive a craft of such great size, upstream and without a wind. But, with the added strength of twenty or thirty folk . . .

Cap'n Potter stood by the helm.

"These are my last orders," he told his company, "as captain of this vessel." He looked round, calmly, though inside him there was an excitement that sang through his every vein, for within an hour it would be known whether the pirate galleon was saved, or lost to the fury of the falls.

"Woo Owl," he said, "fly to each bank, and tell them that when they see our flag run up, they must pull as they have never pulled before."

"Ay, Skipper!"

The Owl was away, beating strongly across the water.

"Cap'n Pirate," said Potter next, "take your pair of crew, and put them to the oars, one for each of them and one for you. Wait for the signal to row."

"Ay, Cap'n," said the Black Otter, and went below with his crew.

"Stripe," said Potter, "Digger Mole—go with them, and take an oar each, and wait. Woo Owl will join you as soon as he gets back."

Without a word the two of them hastened away, down to the benches below, where the long oars were slung through the rowlock-holes in the sides of the galleon.

Woo Owl came flying back, and landed near the helm.

"All ready, Cap'n!"

"Good! There's one oar left, below. Will you take it?"

"I'll take it, ay," said Woo, "and I'll break the blade in the water if needs be . . ." He waddled quickly below, where the others waited for the signal.

Potter-the-Otter turned his head, and looked back, over the stern of the ship, where the water dropped away and plunged with its mighty voice, raising a

silver mist within whose million water-beads there ran a rainbow from the sun. Then he looked forward, over the bows, where the Wild River ran between the gentle banks, upstream to Stricken Oak, past Fallen Elm, to distant Otter's Island.

"That's where you're bound, you good ship," murmured the Islander. "Back to my own bit o' land, where you moored last night. But this time you sail with a different captain, and there'll be a welcome for you when you're safely there . . ."

For a moment more he gazed, his paws trembling with excitement; then quickly he turned and strode to the halyard by the forward mast; and his arms jerked. The flag ran up, unfurling, revealing its

skull and crossbones to the sun. It hung at last, moving
idly, the signal to the shore.

Cap'n Potter's voice rose, roaring:

"Sink those oars—and pull! Take your time from
Cap'n Pirate and row for the Island! *Row!*"

And in the same instant there came from both banks
the shouts of the two leaders on the ropes:

"There goes the flag! Now heave! Heave!
Heave!"

From the sides of the vessel dipped the oars,
ploughing the ripples and pulling, pulling, pulling to
the stroke of the Black Otter——

"*In*—out! *Pull*—out! *One*—out! *Two*—out! *In*—
out! . . ."

"Heave!" came the shouts from the banks, "and *heave—heave—heave!* . . ."

"*In*—out! *Pull*—out!" came the pirate's roar from the oars. Old Stripe heaved his hardest, and his black-and-white brow became furrowed with strenuous wrinkles. Digger Mole pulled and heaved, almost tipping backwards from his seat as the great oar trembled in his paws. Woo Owl, who was sitting behind him, heaved until the feathers stuck out from his brow; and every few moments he gave small Mole a push in the nethers with his feet, for to stop him falling backwards from the seat.

"*One*—out! *Two*—out! *In*—out!"

"*Heave* on that rope! *Heave* on it well! *Heave*—and *heave—again!*"

From the deck of the ship, Cap'n Potter watched the toiling Woodlanders on the shore. He heard their shouts, and heard the roar of the bandit at the oars. He felt, beneath his feet, the trembling of the vessel as her bows felt the straining of the ropes and her beams took the pressure of the oars. He knew, now, that the battle was nearly won. The brink of the Silver Falls was being left in their wake, moment by moment, stroke by stroke, heave by heave on the ropes.

The helm was in his paws, steady. Overhead flew birds, down from the timbers of the land to watch and to cheer the toilers on the banks and the rowers who strained at the blades. It seemed that every folk in the Wood was here, to save the ship that, not very long ago, had entered these waters to harry them.

The Woodland had come to the aid of the foreign

craft; and now, as the oars dipped and drove and the ropes jerked from bank to prow, the Woodland watched the saving of the galleon.

The danger was over, at last. A score of yards astern, the brink receded slowly; and now the current was less fierce; and the journey was easier. The folk along the banks were heaving no longer to the time of their two leaders, but were walking, slowly, bent forward and with the ropes over their shoulders, their feet digging into the ground.

The oars moved more quickly to the bandit's words:

"*In*—out—*in*—out—*pull*—out—*pull*—out!"

The blades drove faster and the water creamed, swirling behind to leave whirling eddies on the surface of the stream. The ropes quivered as the haulers walked faster, pulling up-river at a steady, easy pace. And as they went they broke into a ditty, and their voices lifted to the tops of the sunlit trees where now the leaves moved, trembling to a breeze that was rising from the west.

Cap'n Potter sniffed the air, and became aware of this freshness in it. A slow wind was rising, and he swung round, calling below:

"Cap'n Pirate! Ship oars and get your canvas up!"

The Black Otter came running to the deck, the two Rats with him. The halyards and the tackle clattered while the sailblocks ran and the canvas went up from the base of each great mast, unfolding and filling with the wind that was moving from the west.

"Canvas aloft, Cap'n!" the Black Otter called.

Potter swung the helm, as the river turned through a curve in the widening banks.

"Ship oars," he shouted below.

They came in, rumbling through the rowlocks.

The speed of the vessel did not lessen; and Potter, as he gazed forward, saw that the two hempen cables were slackening, while the folk who hauled on them were running along the banks.

"Woo Owl," he called, "tell them to drop their ropes, on both the banks!"

"Ay, Skipper!" And the Owl rose, dipping in his flight across the waterway. As Potter and the bandit watched, while Stripe and Mole came up from the well of the ship, Woo swooped low over the rope-crews, giving them the message. In a moment the cables dropped, curling into the stream: and still the ship moved on, with scarce a slackening in her pace.

The oars were shipped, the ropes were dropped; the pirate craft moved on, under her own sails. The danger had gone, long ago, and she was safe, together with her crew.

The sun was low, and her great shadow was long in the water behind her stern, when the galleon came to Otter's Island, under her own full canvas and with Potter at the helm.

As the shore of the Island was sighted, Cap'n Potter turned, and looked at the pirate.

"Take your ship, Cap'n Pirate," he said quietly, "for we've done with her now."

The Black Otter came forward, and, as the Woodlander moved aside, his paws rested on the helm, and

felt the trembling of the rudder. He heard Potter-the-
Otter speak again from beside him.

"She's your vessel again, so ye can sail her where
ye will. But if it's Otter's Island that's on your course,
you'll find a welcome there for you, your ship and
your crew . . ."

The pirate moved the helm, slowly in his paws,
and gazed ahead to the shore of the Island that was
looming towards them in the fading light of the sun.

"I—I'm not sure how it is I can thank you, Cap'n
Potter—you and your many friends——"

"Enough of that," said Potter-the-Otter. "We sent
your ship adrift ourselves. Now we've helped save her;
so the score's even."

The Black Otter said nothing for a few moments, as
the great ship neared the Island. Birds had followed
her on her way upstream, and now were wheeling
and circling over the two tall masts. The many folk
along the banks were running still, and now there
came splashes as they began diving in, to swim to the
Isle and look at the ship they had helped to bring to
harbour.

At last the pirate turned to Potter; and what he
said meant as much to Old Stripe, and Digger Mole,
and Woo Owl.

"We didn't have the measure o' you Woodlanders,
when we sailed up your river from the coast. We
thought you were a pack o' white-livered landlubbers,
as we've met so many times before. But—well, if
we'd known you as we do now, as Potter-the-Otter,
and Digger Mole, and Woo Owl, and the Badger from

Badger's Beech, then we'd have come as friends, surely we would."

"Well," said Potter, "you can stay as friends, now that you're here, as far as I'm concerned. Well, Stripey?"

"They can," nodded the Badger quietly.

"Digger?"

"Ay," piped Digger, "if they'll let me play their concertina!"

"Woo?"

"By all means," boomed Woo Owl generously.

The Otter of Otter's Island nodded, and looked at the bandit.

"I suppose," he asked quietly, "I suppose you never saw anything of a small blue sailing-boat, since you arrived in the Wood?"

"Ay," answered the Black Otter, "we did. She lies in that long creek, not far from Winter Marsh. 'Twas in a fit of mischief we took her, and she's safe enough still. We'll fetch her for you, this day, before the sun goes down."

A breath of happiness rose in Potter's furry chest, and he held out his brown paw.

"Then friends you are," he said.

The pirate shook paws with him, warmly.

"We'll raise that other ship o' yours," he went on, "I promise ye that. And mend that water-wheel, and plant the bean-patch again, we will, and gladly!"

Potter-the-Otter gave a sudden chuckle.

"There's one thing you won't do, me bold pirate— and that's return those sacks of flour you took from

Mole-the-Miller, for they're over the Silver Falls by now, along with the rest o' your cargo!"

"And on whose orders, Skipper?" laughed the Black Otter.

"Island coming up, Cap'n!" sang out one of his crew.

He turned, and swung the helm.

"Stand-by to make harbour, then!"

The Water-Rats scuttled, sorting the mooring-ropes.

"Run them sails down!"

Old Stripe and Digger Mole jumped for the halyards, and the rigging-blocks ran with a rattle.

The great ship moved in, with a bubble of beam-wash, as the canvas came billowing down.

"Ropes out and over!"

The Rats jumped, thudding to the shore, running to the mooring-post. Potter-the-Otter threw out the ropes for the Rats to catch and lash.

A cheer went up from the throng of Woodlanders who were now lining the Island shore; and from the sky there swooped the birds, to furl their wings and join the company.

"Welcome to Otter's Island!" cried Potter-the-Otter, and leapt for his homeland soil.

"Ay," came the cheering voices, "welcome to the Wood!"

In the cool of that same evening, when the sun was down and the feasting was at its height in the small snug house on Otter's Isle, the west wind moved through the lands of the Deep Wood, murmuring among the drowsy leaves—of beech and sycamore, elm and oak, and the willows that hung nearby the galleon that lay, motionless, at the Island's shore.

Within her great shadow, a smaller craft rocked upon the ripples, sometimes nudging against the beam of her sister-ship. True to his promise, the Black Otter had brought the small blue *Bunty* home from the creek by Winter Marsh.

From the stone-built house there came the sound of many voices at the feast; and, as Digger Mole struck up a tune on his concertina, the song lifted, to drift above the twilit willow trees:

> ". . . O-o-h, who'd be a Pirate,
> Who'd be a Bandit,
> Who'd be a Robber bold?
> Who wants Treasure, who wants Trove?
> Who wants to Smuggle in a Smuggler's Cove?
> Who wants a Ship full o' Gold?

> "Oh, I'd rather have a Home
> Than sail the Foam,
> Rather have a Pot full o' Tea!
> Sooner see a Hearth and a trim Front-path—
> So this is the Place—
> —fo-o-r
> —Me-e-e!"